10-12-17

See You at Sunset

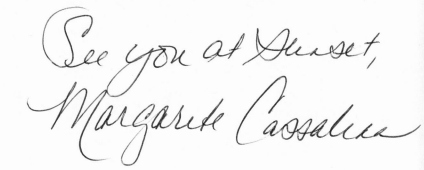

See you at Sunset,
Margarete Cassalina

MARGARETE CASSALINA

SEE YOU AT SUNSET

iUniverse books may be ordered through booksellers or by contacting:

iUniverse
1663 Liberty Drive
Bloomington, IN 47403
www.iuniverse.com
1-800-Authors (1-800-288-4677)

*Because of the dynamic nature of the Internet, any web addresses or links contained in
this book may have changed since publication and may no longer be valid. The views
expressed in this work are solely those of the author and do not necessarily reflect the
views of the publisher, and the publisher hereby disclaims any responsibility for them.*

*Any people depicted in stock imagery provided by Thinkstock are models,
and such images are being used for illustrative purposes only.
Certain stock imagery © Thinkstock.*

ISBN: 978-1-5320-2744-4 (sc)
ISBN: 978-1-5320-2745-1 (hc)
ISBN: 978-1-5320-2746-8 (e)

Library of Congress Control Number: 2017912499

Print information available on the last page.

iUniverse rev. date: 08/17/2017

To Eric, who continually reminds me how bright the future is.

To Jena, who has proven to me that angels exist and that love never ends.

To Marc, who saw in me what no one else ever did. I love you.

1 Room 313

I've been a part of Westchester General Hospital since 1985 when then governor Harry Whitmore held a fancy ribbon-cutting ceremony. It was a regular media frenzy that warm September day. The aster plants that lined the two-acre bluegrass lawn here at 65 Valhalla Circle bloomed the most strikingly rich purple and lavender hues that I had ever seen. The blossoms' fragrant sage scent attracted both bees and hummingbirds to its petals, all hoping to capture a hint of its essence. The old willow tree by the visitors' parking lot provided the perfect shade and space for DJ Dan to set up his equipment. DJ Dan, the voice over the tristate airways, would soon play the music that "holds a memory in a song," as he'd famously say at the top of each listening hour. By noon, the media news outlets had swarmed the front lawn, displaying their sharply dressed news anchors who were awaiting the perfect sound bite to broadcast back to their dedicated viewers.

We certainly looked like something that day. The courtyard was full of red, white, and blue balloons. A huge patriotic-looking "Grand Opening" banner draped across the immense hospital glass entrance way, and of course, all the who's who of the local area were present. There were local senators, state senators, businessmen, and local dignitaries; they all came out to be a part of the monumental ribbon-cutting ceremony that afternoon.

The buzz of the crowd hummed over the noise of the generators that fed the makeshift remote television stations. The tap-tap of the microphone by Governor Whitmore interrupted the murmur of the elected officials who were deciding who would speak next and for how long. We were all excited to be a part of such a groundbreaking event. I remember how Governor Whitmore's face glowed as he basked in the 150-watt camera lighting. During his designated eight-minute speech before the commercial break, he threw out notable catch phrases left and right to the hungry reporters.

"General has the latest and greatest in medical advancements," he boasted to the NBC affiliate.

"We have an unsurpassed, state-of-the-art medical facility," he bragged to the RNN local TV reporter.

He couldn't wait to express to the national public radio station, "We've acquired scientific equipment and technology that is unrivaled in the country."

The reporters ate up every sound bite he gave, and the swarm of bystanders applauded with booming approval.

Well, imagine that. Weren't we the envy.

Governor Whitmore was a polished politician who had perfected his on-air presence by his second term in office. He articulately expressed to the well-dressed CBS news anchorman covering the event that a whopping $20 million was spent to create this "magnificent advancement to health care" that was standing before them. There she stood in all her glory. WGH boasted 2,250 beds, a trauma unit, a critical care unit, an intensive care unit, and a neonatal unit. Exclusive to the area, she even flaunted a separate rehabilitation unit and forty surgical suites and was equipped with her very own helipad.

Governor Whitmore ended his boisterous performance with his last and best sound bite of the day. It was a gift bestowed on the ABC seasoned female reporter who had covered his last election. He looked directly into the camera lens and succinctly stated, "Westchester General Hospital will be known as *the* hospital of choice by all standards to everyone within one hundred miles."

I admit, he was quite convincing that day. Like players before the big game, the coach rallied us, and we bought every word. I was young back then and believed that we could perform miracles. After all, we had all that money could buy. We now had the ability to care for, rebuild, and restore anyone who walked through our new, shiny, chrome automated doors.

Boy, I've seen it all in the last thirty years here at General. I've seen people come in crippled and walk out of their own accord. I've seen broken bones mend and transplants correct the virtually uncorrected. I've seen joyful family reunions, and I've seen atheists come out praying. I've also seen babies die, hearts broken by unforgiving news, and marriages destroyed. I've seen God-fearing people lose faith, and I've seen things no one should ever see, and I've heard sounds I will never forget.

Over the years here at WGH, we've been humbled by humanity and have cursed what we can't control. I don't have that youthful, invincible arrogance anymore; it seems time has weathered me into more of a realist, I guess. Now I keep kind of quiet and just listen mostly and try not to get in the way. It's not so bad, really. I've got a great view of the grand entranceway. I get to see the sunset every night, and

I've gotten to know some special people over the years here in my little corner of the world on 65 Valhalla Circle.

For instance, take little Jenna here. She's only thirteen, and this is her twelfth time being admitted into the hospital. She's one of our regulars, our frequent flyers here at Club Med. All the nurses just eat her up when she walks in the door. She's stolen the hearts of the doctors, the technicians, and housekeeping with that bright smile of hers and her beautiful blue eyes. They gush over her from the minute she walks in and hug her tightly when she's discharged. She usually stays here with us for about three to four weeks each time, sometimes more.

Poor thing, she has cystic fibrosis. A terrible disease to deal with. She was diagnosed here at WGH through newborn screening just days after she was born. It's a genetic disease, one with no cure. Sure, there's medicine and treatments to slow the progressive monster down, but sadly, its only job is to suffocate the lungs with infections and bacteria. Yet she and her mama come in here at least once a year hoping that *this* will be the time we have that miracle she needs. That miracle that will keep her away from this place ... this "hospital of choice by all standards."

*   *   *   *

"Make it like a meat locker in here, George. She likes it nice and cold," Dr. Grazer said to the person on the other end of the phone. He smiled at Jenna and winked.

Jenna smiled in return.

"Uh, room number?" Dr. Grazer glanced over at the door. "Room 313."

Jenna could hear the protest through the phone. Her hearing was still good despite the potential hearing loss, a side effect from the current drug she was on. When Dr.

Grazer had asked if there had been any changes in Jenna's hearing since taking the drug, Mary, her mother, had joked that her daughter now had selective hearing.

"Yes, George." Grazer's head nodded. "I know you don't have temperature control of the individual patient rooms, but see what you can do for me, okay?" He never lost his smile as Jenna heard the persuasion in the voice on the other end.

"Thanks, George. I appreciate the effort." Grazer hung up the phone and gave Jenna a quick wink.

Jenna giggled and gave him two thumbs-up as the nurse took her vitals.

Sara, Jenna's nurse, unwrapped the small, blue blood pressure cuff from Jenna's arm. "It's a good thing I brought my sweater today, sweetie. I didn't know you were coming in."

"I'm glad you're here today, Miss Sara," Jenna said. "It'd be a total drag if *You-Know-Who* was my admitting nurse." Jenna smirked. Sara let out a faint giggle.

"*You-Know-Who*," Sara said, mimicking Jenna's tone, "is off today and tomorrow."

"Yes!" Jenna cheered.

Sara smiled at Jenna and turned her attention turned toward Dr. Grazer, her tone more serious. "Blood pressure is 107/68, temp is 98.4 degrees, weight sixty-three pounds, height fifty-five inches," Sara said. Then her voice fell a bit lower. "And um the pulse oximeter reads … eighty-nine O2." Sara finished writing the numbers on Jenna's chart and handed it off to Dr. Grazer.

"Well, kiddo, you finally made the chart," Dr. Grazer exclaimed. "Fifth percentile on weight, tenth percentile on height. But I'm not liking the eighty-nine oxygen number." Dr. Grazer frowned for a moment. "You're going to have to do continuous oxygen until we can get those numbers back up. Deal?" He tousled her long blonde hair.

"Two liters?" Nurse Sara asked.

"Yes. We'll start with that and see how she responds," Dr. Grazer answered as he flipped the pages in Jenna's chart.

Sara handed Jenna the coil of rubber tubing and began to adjust Jenna's bed lower. Jenna expertly placed the nasal cannula in her nose and draped the tubing around her ears. She then attached the hose to the socket in the wall and turned the green oxygen knob to 2. Then she jumped out of bed, the tubing draped around her, and grabbed the backpack of goodies she had brought from home.

"Hey, Ma, you want to play Rummy or Boggle?" Jenna questioned without missing a beat. Searching the bag, she pulled out a deck of cards and a notebook.

"Either one, honey. You pick. Just give me a couple of minutes to go over your admission with Miss Sara and Dr. Grazer, okay?" Mary answered. She stood next to Dr. Grazer as he wrote in Jenna's chart. Her eyes fixed on what he was writing down as her hands nervously tucked her overgrown bangs back behind her ears. Hospital admissions were common for Mary, yet each admittance felt like a punch in the gut and another failing defeat as a mother.

"Fine," Jenna said in a huff, plopping her small frame back on the bed and clicking on the TV. When she let out a couple of deep hacking coughs, Mary turned her attention back to her daughter, took out a bottle of blue Gatorade from her purse, and handed it to Jenna. Jenna unscrewed the cap and took a long gulp.

"Jenna?" Grazer asked. "Is that how your cough has been sounding lately?"

"Yeah, kind of," she said and then took another sip of her Gatorade.

Jenna's eyes never left the TV screen as she continued to click through the stations. She finally stopped at one of her favorite shows, *Full House*.

"Yes!" she said. Though it was in syndicated reruns, she didn't care, she loved the series. She took the stiff white pillow and shoved it behind her back and adjusted the bed higher. She put the Gatorade on the hospital tray, next to the deck of cards and notebook. She reached again for the backpack and pulled out a large bag of peanut M&Ms. Engrossed in the show, Jenna began to giggle; her giggling triggered a series of deep, raspy coughs. She reached for her Gatorade, took another few sips, and leaned back against the pillow. No one even noticed that the air conditioner vents had kicked on and cool air began to fill the room.

Mary anxiously looked back at Dr. Grazer. He motioned toward the door, and they stepped outside. Mary waited patiently as Dr. Grazer shut the door. "Mrs. Rutherford, we'll take Jenna down for x-rays this afternoon and get her IV started in about an hour. Her cultures show two different strains of pseudomonas, so we'll be hitting them pretty hard with IV antibiotics. I'd like the dietitian to come up and see you later this week to try to get her weight up."

Mary nervously bit her bottom lip as she pushed her bangs back again.

"Okay. That sounds like a plan," she said. Though her head nodded as he spoke, her attention and eyes stared at the floor. Her thoughts were calculating the length of the stay this time, her mind wondering how bad Jenna's lungs were.

Grazer settled back into his caring way. He gently placed his hand on Mary's shoulder, and her attention quickly shifted back to him. His green eyes softened as his tone remained solemn.

"It's going to take awhile to get it all under control this time," he said.

Mary studied his face for answers. She could gauge the severity by Dr. Grazer's tone and demeanor. He seemed more serious than normal. Her stomach knotted.

"Mrs. Rutherford, you better plan on being here at least three weeks, probably more."

*   *   *   *

That's the way it goes here. Some stay awhile. Some go. Jenna knows this place so well she hardly puts up much of a fight anymore. She'll settle in quickly, dinner will come up soon, and the room will get nice and cold just the way she likes it. She's special to us here at General, and we all keep an eye on her … especially me.

It's what I do.

My name is Alex. This is my home.

I'm Room 313.

2 Peanut M&Ms

"C'mon, Ma, fair's fair ... pay up!" Jenna said as she extended her hand for payment. She sat cross-legged in her jeans and T-shirt on the hospital bed. The oxygen tubing was looped around her ears and dangled down in front of her slender body. It had been six days since she was admitted to Westchester General; she was now on the autopilot part of her hospitalization, as Dr. Grazer would say. During this autopilot time, not much would change in her hospital care routine. She'd get her two IV antibiotics every six hours, her thirty-minute breathing treatments three times a day, her double order of fattening and salty meals for breakfast, lunch, and dinner, and daily blood work that would check for toxicity levels due to all her medication and see if her blood sugars were elevated. This autopilot time would allow the medicine and treatments to kick in so the doctor could see what results presented in Jenna's overall health. Jenna's appetite had not changed much, but the blue tint of her lips had noticeably faded. On day two of her admission, Dr. Grazer had upped her oxygen requirement to three liters, yet her O2 levels rarely stayed above ninety-three. Despite the long week of tests, x-rays, around-the-clock IV antibiotics, and constant medical attention, Jenna's disposition remained upbeat and remarkably witty.

"Really!" Mary sat at the foot of Jenna's bed, her eyes in disbelief at the four aces Jenna just victoriously laid across the center of the hospital tray. Mary threw up her hands in animated despair. "That's six wins in a row, four bags of peanut M&Ms, and one trip to Barnes and Noble to get the latest edition of Carrie Brigg's Long Distant Sister series. If I didn't know you any better, young lady, I'd swear you were holding those aces up your sleeve!" Mary rolled the hospital tray away so she could get up and retrieve her purse.

"Looks like I interrupted at the right time." Dr. Grazer smiled as he walked in the room. "What are the stakes today?"

"Peanut M&Ms!" Jenna said. "One for every ten points, and I'm up four bags! Want to play?"

"Sure, I think I have time for a quick game later today after I finish rounds." Dr. Grazer grinned. His genuine sincerity was obvious.

"Make sure you bring plenty of M&Ms. I'm on a winning streak," Jenna said excitedly as she popped a few of her wins into her mouth.

Mary had suggested that they play for peanut M&Ms. She'd always try anything to get calories into her tiny daughter. She had been trying for years to hide calories in Jenna's food to get her weight up, but no matter what Mary tried, Jenna would just complain how her belly would feel sick or too full every time she ate. Mary would hide extra butter and heavy cream in Jenna's mac and cheese. Mary even bought that expensive ice cream that had over three hundred calories a quarter cup in any and every flavor Jenna requested. Mary often bought those highly caloric frozen dinners that Jenna begged for at the grocery store, but after a few bites, the pain would return, and the food would go untouched. Every time Jenna would complain about her stomach, Mary would try something else to appease her daughter's ever-changing appetite. It was surprising that with all the calories and food constantly rotating in the house, Mary could never gain weight either. She chalked up her 125 pounds to nerves and the constant knot in her stomach.

Dr. Grazer closed Jenna's chart he'd just read and pushed aside the half-eaten double-order breakfast tray of pancakes, eggs, and bacon. He placed the chart down on the counter and scrubbed his hands in the sink, then ripped a sheet of paper towels from the dispenser and looked back at Jenna.

"Let's have a listen to those lungs today." He finished drying his hands and reached for his stethoscope. He looked down at the ground, concentrating on what his ears registered through the stethoscope.

As Dr. Grazer moved the stethoscope's chest piece around Jenna's back, Mary watched as Jenna took a deep breath in. Jenna had learned over the years when to breathe deeply and when to just breathe regularly. She had done this a million times. Nobody said a word as they awaited Dr. Grazer's professional assessment. After a few minutes, he removed the stethoscope from his ears and rested it back around his neck.

"Well, everything sounds the same," Dr. Grazer stated.

Mary sighed, knowing that meant the antibiotics weren't doing what they were supposed to—the infection in her lungs was still actively growing.

"And," Grazer continued, "according to the x-rays, it looks like you still have some chronic inflammation in your upper right lobe, and the Aspergillus culture is showing a very persistent strain. The antibiotics don't seem to be doing what I'd hoped, so we're going to switch things up a bit, okay?" Dr. Grazer directed his words toward Jenna, who was looking intently back at him.

He always spoke directly to Jenna during his scheduled office appointments, which Mary appreciated. He'd told her that no matter how old the patient was, they needed to have some responsibility and understanding of what was going on regarding their health and wellness. Of course, Mary was always right there next to her daughter, transcribing every word Dr. Grazer said into her notebook so she'd be sure to get it right later that evening when she explained what had happened during the appointment to her husband, Jim.

Dr. Grazer often told Jenna that it was all about her anyway and that Mom was just her personal driver, the backup really, until she got her license. She'd always giggle at his humor.

This time Dr. Grazer turned his attention toward Mary, who was scribbling down everything he said into her three-inch blue binder. His tone became serious.

"Mary, you may want to bring Jim in later today." He paused. "Jenna's weight hasn't budged in eighteen months, and Dr. Mendoza and I feel it's time for her to get that feeding tube we've talked about."

"What? No!" Jenna protested. "No, Mommy! I promise I'll eat more—see?" Jenna cried as she popped a handful of peanut M&Ms into her mouth.

"Please, Mommy. No!"

A feeding tube? Mary held back her dismay. The look on her daughter's face nearly broke her heart. Mary felt she had completely let her daughter down. All her tricks, her bribery, her sneaking calories into her daughter's food couldn't prevent this moment. She let out a heavy, involuntary sigh to release the weight of her guilt.

"Sweetie, it's not because you're not doing your best, really." Dr. Grazer tried to console her. "You know we have been talking about this for quite some time now." His tone softened as he sat next to her on the bed. His eyes looked directly into hers. "It's just that all this junk in your lungs is taking all the calories and energy you eat. You just can't possibly eat the four to five thousand calories your body needs to grow. And you need to grow big and strong, right? I mean, someone's gotta drive your mom around when she's old," he said, trying to lighten the mood.

Tears rolled down her flushed cheeks as she nodded. "Just make the junk go away," Jenna demanded as she looked up at Dr. Grazer.

"Honey, we're trying. I'm doing everything I can." Dr. Grazer put his arm around Jenna and kissed the top of her head. Jenna leaned into his shoulder, trying to hide her tears. Dr. Grazer gave her a quick, tight hug. At the last hospitalization, he had told Mary that in his thirty years of medical practice, there was just something special about Jenna that tugged at his heart. With his arm still around Jenna, he let out a long exhale as if changing a thought in his head. He gave Jenna another quick squeeze and stood up.

He looked back at Mary and said, "I've ordered a switch in her antibiotics and added Sporanox to her meds for the Aspergillus. Dr. Mendoza will be in later today to discuss the details of the surgery with you." He glanced at Jenna, then back at Mary. "Will Mr. Rutherford be able to make it by four o'clock?"

"I'm sure he will." Mary felt defeated as she stared at her watch. "He should be off work by now. I'll give Jim a call."

13

3 Hospitals and Chocolate Pudding

enna's lunch tray came up at 12:30 p.m., the same time her nurse carrying her afternoon IV meds walked in. Jenna uncovered her lunch only to discover that her lunch was not what she had ordered earlier that day. She let out a long sigh to get the attention of her nurse, but it went unnoticed. Jenna let out another longer sigh.

"Yes, dear? Is that your way to get my attention?" said the elderly, heavyset nurse. Her gray hair was pinned back in a bun and fastened with a half-dozen bobby pins. She wore no makeup, and her dry lips often cracked when she spoke. Jenna noticed that her breath always smelled like a eucalyptus cough drop.

"There's no chocolate pudding," Jenna said.

"Well, dear, this isn't a five-star restaurant," Jenna's most disliked daytime nurse said. Jenna had forgotten her real name and just referred to her as Daytime Nurse, Nurse, or her favorite, *You-Know-Who*. Daytime Nurse never worked nights or weekends, and Jenna was pretty sure she'd been a nurse for at least a hundred years. She always wore a dowdy, wrinkled, off-white, almost gray uniform dress. The off-white color showed its contrast to the crisp white stockings and white rubber-soled shoes that she wore. The front buttons had been replaced over the years, and none of them matched. Jenna often wondered why she worked with children; it was clear she didn't like them.

"There's no Zagat rating here, honey. You get what is deemed appropriate by your dietician."

"I know, but—"

"But," she interrupted, "this is what was ordered this morning when food service came up to ask you what *you'd* like. See?" Her tone was always so condescending. She held the printed slip of paper with the number 313 written at the top.

> Room: #313
> June 12, 2016—Lunch
> Diet: Pediatric Cystic Fibrosis
> Doctor: Ben Grazer, MD
> Dietician: Jen Moore, RDN

Jenna rolled her eyes. *Wow*, Jenna thought. Daytime Nurse could actually read without the glasses that always hung around her neck.

"Well, umm, I'm *supposed* to get double orders. I have CF, ya know," Jenna retorted.

"Don't get snappy with me."

Did she just say snappy? I mean, who says that? I wonder if Daytime Nurse knows television is in color now.

"Yes, ma'am," Jenna answered. "But since I'm an only child, I'm kind of used to the undivided attention."

"Well, *dear*, I have four other patients, and you'll just have to wait your turn."

"Okay. Thank you," Jenna replied. "But when it's my turn, can I get a couple of chocolate puddings instead of the ice cream with my lunch?" Jenna smiled. "And this morning,

I asked for spaghetti with meatballs with extra cheese, not this." Jenna looked over at her lunch tray; she guessed it was supposed to be sliced turkey and mashed potatoes, but it was some kind of semi-green mystery meat and a packaged potato product. *Ugh.*

"Now, Jenna, you know we don't have any chocolate pudding here at General," Daytime Nurse said.

"Really?" Jenna asked, deliberately sounding surprised. "But I had it yesterday. In fact, I *always* have it here at General."

"I'm sorry, *dear*," Daytime Nurse snipped back. "Maybe your mother brought it in. I'll go see about getting you your ice cream like everyone else."

"And my double order of spaghetti?"

"I'll see what I can do."

Jenna mimicked her under her breath but said "Thank you" loud enough for Daytime Nurse to hear before the door closed.

About five minutes later, there was a knock at her door.

"Yes?" Jenna asked, knowing full well the knock-and-walk-in policy at General. No one really cared about patient privacy, but they tried to give the impression they did. Even though most people knocked as they opened the door, no one actually waited to be invited in.

There was another knock.

"Hello?" Jenna said. Her curiosity was piqued. "The door is open. I mean, there aren't any locks here anyway."

Oswin slowly opened the door. "Well, hello, Miss Jenna. Mind if me come in?" he said in a heavy Jamaican accent. "Me need to clean da room."

"Hey, Mr. Oswin. What's up? Wah gwaan?" Jenna asked.

"Lawd 'ave mercy, Miss Jenna." His smiled widened. "Yuh sup'm else." He was an older man, but it was hard to tell how old exactly; he had a few gray strands in his black, coarse hair. His frame was slight and bent, and his skin was deep, deep black. His teeth shone white against his warm red lips. And his smile made Jenna's face light up.

"Hey, Mr. Oswin, you play Rummy?" Jenna asked her friend.

"Nah, child." Oswin began mopping the floor next to her bed. Jenna smelled the sharp lemon and pine scents mixed with ammonia with each stoke of the mop. Jenna studied his face, his hands, his body as he swayed with the ebb and flow of the mop. He seemed so content, so at home. Maybe that's why she felt so calm around him. She wondered what his story was.

"You got any kids, Mr. Oswin? Any grandkids?" she quickly added. "Hey, Mr. Oswin, how old are you anyway?" she innocently questioned.

"Mi wurd, Miss Jenna, you be excited today," Oswin said.

"Awe, it's just 'cause *You-Know-Who* is on today, and I just wanted someone fun to talk to." She motioned her head toward the door

"Ah, me see, child."

Jenna watched him as he pushed his mop back and forth, whistling to himself. He always seemed calm and content. Jenna couldn't remember a time when he wasn't at the hospital.

"Mr. Oswin, how long have you been here?" Jenna questioned.

"Ah dog hair less than thirty years, me guess," he said, never stopping the sway of the mop. "Me born in Kingston, Jamaica, child. Long, long time ago. And me be working me way nort ever since."

Jenna thought about his answer and questioned, "Why on earth would you leave the sun of Jamaica to come here?" She looked out her window at the dreary gray sky. It was cool for June, and the skies had rained for days. She could see the willow tree sway in the wind as the rain drenched the ground. New York was usually pretty this time of year but not today. Jenna blamed Daytime Nurse for the nasty weather and let out a humph.

She turned back to her friend. "Hey, Mr. Oswin, isn't their slogan 'Come to Jamaica, Mon'?" She paused. "'Cause I'm pretty sure we don't have 'Come to Westchester General, Mon.'" She laughed.

Oswin's smile widened as he looked over at his little friend. "You be sup'm, child."

She giggled again.

"Yeah, but really, Mr. Oswin. Why are you here?" Jenna genuinely wanted to know.

"Some tings be better left unsaid," he said quietly.

"Huh?" Jenna asked.

"Ah, child, you ask too many questions. Me here because it where I need to be."

The door opened, and Daytime Nurse walked in, her hands full.

"See?" Jenna said to Oswin. "No privacy."

He just shook his head, looked down at the floor to hide his smile, and continued his mopping.

Daytime Nurse was focused on what was in her hands; she didn't even hear Jenna.

"Okay, we need to get your meds running," Daytime Nurse said. She put her glasses on, and they rested on the tip of her nose. She concentrated as she read the medicine bags that were in her hand. She placed one on the counter and hung the other one on the hook of Jenna's IV pole. She reached in her pocket and took out a clear syringe.

"Fine," Jenna said. "But my IV is a little sluggish today. Can you push the flush in slowly?"

"Sure," Daytime Nurse said.

"And can you run the Tobra a little slower too? It's starting to hurt," Jenna added as she lightly touched her arm just above where the IV was taped underneath with clear Tegaderm tape.

Daytime Nurse was focused on her job at hand and hadn't listened to Jenna. She pushed the syringe flush at her normal speed. There was no concern that the force of the saline burned as it coursed into Jenna's veins. Jenna winced in pain as the saline flush entered her bloodstream.

"Ouch!" she said. Even though it stung, Jenna knew better than to move her arm and held it still as it burned.

"Oh come now," Daytime Nurse said. "It's only saline for Cripe's sake!"

Jenna scowled. *"Cripe's?* What is that?"

"Never you mind."

Daytime Nurse wiped her IV cap with squares of alcohol wipes, then attached the end of the plastic tubing to her now sterilized catheter. She skillfully threaded the machine with the rubber tubing and pushed a bunch of buttons. The machine started to turn the wheel, and the medicine started dripping through the tubing, entering Jenna's veins.

"Hey, that's too fast!" Jenna cried out.

"Oh, please," Daytime Nurse said. "It's the normal speed. You're just being difficult."

"Don't be messin wid a skinny calf. Da bull could be watchin," Oswin said under his breath in barely a whisper. Oswin finished mopping and rested the mop back in the dirty water bucket. He opened up two yellow plastic caution signs; one he left in the room a few feet from Jenna's bed, and the other one he placed right outside the door.

"Fine. But now it will run longer," said Daytime Nurse, looking at Jenna. "I'll slow it down to ninety, and you'll be hooked to it about an hour more." She hit a few buttons on the IV pump, and the wheel started to turn slower.

"Better?" she snapped.

"Yes," Jenna said. "Besides, where else am I going?" Her hands directed her attention around the empty room.

"Well, some of us have things to do today." Daytime Nurse scowled. Her disapproving eyes looked at Jenna while she gathered the ripped alcohol pads and threw them in the garbage.

"Thank you," Jenna said, not meaning it.

"You're welcome," Daytime Nurse said, not meaning it.

As the aged nurse turned her back to walk out of the room, Jenna stuck her tongue out. Just then, her mother walked in, passing Daytime Nurse in the doorway, holding a McDonald's bag that smelled of hot fries and cheeseburgers.

Mary caught her daughter's gesture. "Hey, now." Her tone was stern. Jenna just shrugged her shoulders as the door closed behind Daytime Nurse.

"You're a doll, Ma!" Jenna's face lit up seeing the bag in Mary's hand. "I'm starving—and look what they sent up." She motioned at the tray of slimy sliced turkey, overcooked peas, and a scoop of yellow mashed potatoes that had started to form a hard coating. "No chocolate pudding either. Just this." She held up a small Styrofoam cup of melting vanilla ice cream.

"And no double order, either!"

Mary handed off the McDonald's bag to Jenna, who immediately reached into the bag and shoved a handful of hot fries into her mouth.

Her mouth full, Jenna mumbled, "Who's on the board for nurse tonight? This one's gotta go fly her broomstick back to 1912."

"Jenna." Mary's reprimanding voice was back.

"Ma, come on, seriously? She doesn't even like children, and who doesn't like me?" She smiled as she reached for another handful of fries.

Mary just smiled, shook her head at her daughter's wit, and sipped her coffee.

They both heard elevated voices and loud commotion from the hallway. Jenna raised her eyebrows. Mary walked over and slightly opened the door. Her eyes widened, and she covered her mouth as she looked back at Jenna.

"What's going on, Ma?" Jenna asked. Her mom held the door open wider so Jenna could see the hallway.

Daytime Nurse apparently had not paid attention to Oswin's yellow caution sign on the floor. She had tripped over it and landed butt first in the dirty mop bucket, knocking both herself and the bucket to the floor. There was a gathering around her trying to help her up.

"What in God's name is that doing there!" Jenna heard her yell from the hallway.

"Well, Gertrude, you did trip over the caution sign." Another familiar nurse's voice answered.

Mary shut the door and walked back over to Jenna, who was already covering her mouth and giggling.

"I'm just glad she's okay." Mary clearly tried to sound concerned, but Jenna saw she was covering a smile. Jenna was now in a full belly laugh.

There was a knock at the door, and as the door opened, another nurse popped her head in. "I'm sorry, little lady," she said. "You are going to have to deal with me for the rest of the day. It seems Nurse Gertrude had a little mishap today and needed to take the rest of the afternoon off."

"Okay. Thanks, Miss Ellen," Jenna said. "I hope she's all right," Jenna added, barely containing her giggle.

"Oh, nothing a change of dry clothes, an icepack, and

an afternoon off can't fix." She smiled back at Jenna. "I'll be back in about thirty minutes to check on your meds." She gave Mary a friendly wave and shut the door.

Mary and Jenna just looked at each other and busted out laughing. After Jenna finished most of her fries and half the cheeseburger, Jenna started to shuffle a deck of cards.

"Ready for another game, Ma?" she asked.

"Sure."

They played two rounds of Rummy when another tray of food arrived. There was no printed slip, but there were double orders of Jenna's favorite, spaghetti and meatballs with extra cheese, and two chocolate pudding cups.

Mary's cell phone rang. She glanced down and said to Jenna, "I'll just step out and be right back." Jenna nodded, reaching for a few peanut M&Ms.

* * * *

Mary stepped around the yellow caution sign and headed for a corner of the hospital hallway. It was Jim calling her back. She had been unable to reach him earlier and had just left him a voicemail.

"Where were you?" she said impatiently. She paced the tile floor, her hand tight on the phone, the other pushing her bangs back. He spoke briefly as she walked down the hallway. "Yes, Jim at 4:00 p.m. Dr. Mendoza would like to speak with us about Jenna." She paused, her voice choking back, "Yes, they want to do the surgery ..." She closed her eyes and took a deep breath. "Tomorrow, Jim." She paused. "Yes, tomorrow."

She listened a few moments and then spoke again, annoyance clear in her voice. "Yes, I know, Jim, I know ... but ..." She paused as she listened. "Jim, listen, they'll be here at four." Her voice sounded stronger, as if she were gaining strength by holding back tears.

"You think I don't know that, Jim? I tried for years ..." Her voice trailed off.

"Jim, they'll be here this afternoon. I expect you to be here at four." She paused for a moment and listened.

"Fine."

She started walking back toward the room. "Of course you can talk to her. I was just in the hallway. She doesn't need to hear all this, Jim."

Mary and Jim married the first week in June 2002, and Jenna was born in March the following year. After losing out on a professional baseball career, Jim joined the Yorktown police force. Still the athlete, Jim spent hours running cross-country, sweating out his anxieties and fears rather than talking them out. As Jenna's disease progressed, his anxieties increased, and he ran more and talked less. As Mary dealt with Jim not being a part of Jenna's hospital care, her own anger and frustration grew, but so did her strength. As her daughter's health declined, Mary found refuge in reading her novels and the sympathetic ear of her younger sister, Mallory.

Her energy gathered, she pasted a cheerful expression on her face as she walked back into room 313.

"Hello, Madre!" Jenna waved at her mother.

Mary looked over at her daughter and raised her eyebrows. "Yes?"

"Ah, there you are—oh, sorry, I didn't know you were on the phone."

"That's okay. It's Daddy. He wants to talk to you."

"Cool!" She scraped the last bit of chocolate from her second chocolate pudding and tossed it into the garbage across the room. "She shoots! She scores! And the crowd goes wild, final score 23-0."

Mary smiled at Jenna, who now had both arms straight up, fists waving as if she had just won the NBA playoffs. "Here you go, LeBron." Mary handed Jenna the phone.

By 3:45 p.m., Mary had gone downstairs to the cafeteria and filled her coffee mug for the third time, cried in the elevator on the way up to the third floor, and regained her composure before she walked into the room. She was ready to lose yet another hand of cards to her daughter while waiting for Jim.

*   *   *   *

I've been here long enough to know it's the little things that make a world of difference in this place. It's a friendly smile, a chocolate pudding cup, even a well-placed caution sign that can make a lasting impact. It doesn't matter who you are, even if you're a You-Know-Who, but you had better make an effort because LeBron James just might be sitting crossed-legged on a hospital bed wearing jeans.

4 The Surgery

The next morning, Mary and Jim sat nervously with their coffees in the pediatric surgical waiting room on the second floor for over three hours. Jenna had gone in a little after seven, and it was almost ten thirty when a cheery, freckled-face nurse popped her head in the door. She pulled down her surgical mask.

"Dr. Mendoza said everything went well. She'll be out to speak with you shortly."

Mary and Jim jumped to their feet and walked toward the door.

"How's Jenna?" Mary asked.

"She did great and is in recovery now with Dr. Mendoza. She shouldn't be much longer."

"Thank you," Jim said.

The nurse gave a kind smile and shut the door.

Mary reached for Jim's hand, and he gave it a squeeze.

"She did great," he said.

"Thank God." Mary let out a sigh. "Dr. Grazer said that Dr. Ava Mendoza, the chief pediatric surgeon, was his only option for this surgery. He said he'd probably assist her and do a bronchoscopy while Jenna was under general anesthesia. I wonder how that went." She tucked her bangs back and looked at Jim for a response.

"I'm sure it went fine. She just said Jenna did great."

The door opened, and both Dr. Mendoza, the surgeon, and Dr. Grazer stepped into the waiting room, masks dangling on their chests. Mary held her breath as she waited for them to speak.

"The surgery was a success," Mendoza said with a smile. Her hands were small, her nails manicured and smooth. Mary looked at her own hands, dry and cracked from all the hand washing she'd been doing.

"We were able to surgically insert her gastrostomy tube, her G-tube, through her abdomen, leaving a 2.5-inch temporary tubing as access until the site heals, which should take about two weeks. Then we can easily replace it with a flush, low-profile 12 French Mic-Key button. Of course we'll take her down for x-rays then to make sure it's all properly placed."

"While Ava finished up," Dr. Gazer interjected, "I took the opportunity to go in and clean out her lungs as best as possible. They were pretty filled," he said, looking at Jim. Jim nodded as he allowed Dr. Grazer to continue.

"I got some really good sputum samples while I was in there."

Mary stared intently as she listened to what they were saying. This was Jenna's second bronchoscopy this year, and all she could think was that Dr. Grazer had scraped, sucked, and lavaged Jenna's lungs from the inside while she lay there motionless on the outside.

The goal of the bronchoscopy after the surgery was to get a deep sputum sample and to temporarily clear the thick mucus out of her lungs. The last five bronchoscopies hadn't kept the mucus at bay for more than a few months. She wondered how soon Jenna would have to go through the procedure again.

Grazer said, "We sent the cultures to be retested against the antibiotics. I'll let you know as soon as the results are in."

"Thank you," Mary said, looking at Dr. Grazer. "When can we go see her?"

"She's just getting set up in recovery," Dr. Mendoza said. "Ellen should be in to get you in about ten minutes. I'll go back there and check now." She stepped toward the door and left.

Grazer waited in the silence. He looked at Mary and Jim a moment. "She did great." He sounded assuring. "Ava was able to place the G-tube off to left and right below her ribcage. It's the least noticeable spot and the most comfortable." His tone was warm and comforting, but his face looked worn and tired for so early in the day. His reddish-blond hair hid the gray strands that scattered in his waves. He waited another moment before he placed his hand on Jim's shoulder. "I'll check in on her later today once she's back up in her room. Right now I've got to scrub in for another patient."

"Oh, of course." Mary apologized for taking his time. "Thank you."

"She'll be just fine." Dr. Grazer gave a quick wave as he turned around and walked out the door. In a matter of seconds, he popped his head back in. "I see Ellen walking down the hallway. She'll take you to go see Jenna."

"Oh good," Mary said as she grabbed her bag.

"Mary, you want these coffees?" Jim asked. But Mary had already left the waiting room to meet Nurse Ellen in the hallway.

Mary watched as Jenna began to come out of anesthesia. She moaned as she tried to understand where she was, her eyes searching the room. Mary jumped up from her chair and got within a foot of Jenna's face so she could clearly see her.

"It's Mommy, honey. I'm right here," she said softly as she kissed her warm cheek.

Jenna's eyes were glassy as she looked back at Mary. She tried to speak, but the oxygen mask covered her nose and mouth.

"Shh, honey," Mary said. "Just relax and sleep. Dr. Grazer said you did great." Mary kissed her forehead.

Jenna looked around the room until she saw Jim. She smiled and gave him a thumbs-up. He smiled and returned the gesture with both his thumbs up.

"Great job, slugger," he said.

Her eyes rolled back as she fell back asleep, Mary still holding her hand.

"It's the anesthesia," the nurse in green scrubs explained. "She'll be in and out for the next hour or so. It's normal. You can go back and sit down if you'd like. She'll probably be sleeping for a while."

Mary nodded in agreement. She had been through this before, and she hated that she knew that. She hated that she had to put her daughter through this. She hated that she had failed her.

The recovery room was full of nurses and doctors going about their workday. There was a quick pace, but no one seemed to be in a rush. They tended to the needs of their patients as the visitors anxiously watched. The bright florescent lights reflected off the newly buffed tiled floor. The incessant beeps of the monitors went unnoticed by everyone. The commotion in the recovery room provided a constant hum of controlled chaos. Orders called. Cabinets opening. Drawers shutting. Gauze pads tearing. Gurneys screeching. Voices muffled. Alarms beeping. Phones ringing. Rubber soles squeaking.

Jenna's legs were covered with heated blankets to offset the chill in the room, and her stomach was wrapped with bandages from the surgery. Rubber tubes snaked out from underneath it, the gauze bandages leading to plastic bags that hung on a hook at the foot of her bed. The bags were being filled with droplets of blood mixed with green mucus. Mary stared at the bag as it filled. She watched as her daughter slept while her body discarded the diseased fluids. Mary's eyes followed the multiple wires, an assortment of red, blue, and green, that led from Jenna to a loudly beeping monitor that hung high above, to the right of Jenna's bed. Some of the wires were taped to her chest, measuring her heart rate, and one wire ran down her hand and made her right pointer finger have a red glow, like ET, Jenna had once said. The small blue cuff wrapped around her leg inflated every fifteen minutes, measuring her blood pressure, heart rate, and pulse.

Jenna looked so small and frail wrapped in her blankets, her face almost as pale as the white pillowcase.

Mary held Jenna's left unobstructed hand while Jim sat in the beige resin chair at the foot of the bed, his eyes locked on the monitor, constantly criticizing the low oxygen numbers registered on the screen. "Why are they so low?"

Mary dismissed him, keeping her focus on Jenna.

The nurse in green scrubs leaned over her bed, adjusting a wire. "Once she is fully awake and her vitals are good enough, we can get her back upstairs to her room." Mary could smell a trace of perfume as she moved about the room. Mary liked when the nurses didn't smell so sterile. The light flowery scent reminded Mary that hospitals were filled with real people with real emotions and real scents, not just bleach and an uncaring, unapproachable staff.

Mary and Jim looked at her as she continued to transcribe all the numbers from the monitor above to the sheet of paper she held in her hand. She then slipped the paper into her front pocket. With ease, the nurse swiftly changed the soiled bags at the end of the bed with fresh, empty ones. She then pressed a few buttons on the noisy monitor, and they beeped on command with each press. Jim stood up abruptly, as if he were being polite at a dinner table, nervous he was in the way while she cared for his daughter. Mary gazed at him, a bit annoyed but knowing he just couldn't sit still.

Mary anxiously asked the nurse, "Do you have any idea how long that will be?"

The nurse gave them a gentle, well-rehearsed reply. "Jenna's in control of that. We'll just have to wait for her to let us know when."

* * * *

There are times when we feel helpless and our hearts hurt, when we just don't know what to do, when prayers don't seem to resonate strongly enough in the direction of "doing something." That's when you know the best thing you can do is just be there. Listen. Hold a hand. Sit in the un-silence. Sometimes there are places you never want to be, and sometimes those places are the only place you need to be. So you sit. You wait.

Don't worry. Someone will always let you know when it's time to leave.

5 Mr. Bunny and the Coat

*T*hree floors below room 313, the emergency room waiting area swirled with noise and activity. The clock on the wall ticked with each second. The TV was on, and the weatherman was talking about the heat wave that had hit the area after such a cool and rainy start to June. A young couple was sitting in one corner, their faces consumed with nervous emotion.

"I swear to God, Tommy, this is all your fault!" Amy Waal screamed at her husband. "Emily never would have been here if you weren't on that damn computer. How could you not notice that she opened the front door! I mean really! Is that … that … that …" Amy's hands waved wildly in the air, "that *whatever* it is on the damn screen more important than watching your own daughter?"

Tommy held Emily's little pink and green jacket in his hands. He didn't blink. He didn't move. He just sat there, staring at the stained hospital carpet under his feet. Around them, the waiting room buzzed with conversation and activity.

"Damn it, Tommy, I'm talking to you! Are you even listening to me?" Amy stared at Tommy for a few seconds, waiting for a response. In disgust, she threw her purse on the floor and plopped hard into the worn waiting room chair by the entrance. She buried her face in her hands and started to cry.

Tommy was only able to just sit in the hard plastic chair. He stared blindly into nothing, his mind just replaying the last hour of his life—their lives—in his head, over and over. It took only a split second to open a portal to another world in Warcraft. It was only a few seconds. Emily had been sitting right next to him holding her *Ten Little Rabbits* book, reading to Mr. Bunny.

"See, look at me, Daddy. I'm Mommy." Emily's soft voice held a faint lisp.

Tommy looked over to see Emily sitting in Amy's recliner, engrossed in her favorite rabbit book that was naturally upside down. She held it firmly as she concentrated on each word, sliding her four-year-old finger quickly over each letter as she narrated the memorized story to Mr. Bunny, her stuffed sidekick.

Tommy gave her a quick smile and went back to finishing his Business Management online class assignment: "Global Competitive Strategy"—Chapter 10: Controlling International Strategies and Operations.

He'd been taking the accelerated online classes to get his degree quicker. Once he completed his degree, he could get the raise he needed. School came easy to him, and maintaining his 3.64 GPA wasn't difficult, but this particular summer class was the most challenging by far. The professor demanded a lot from his students, and Tommy always delivered.

There.

Done.

He took a quick glance at his phone: 11:47 a.m.

Emily was still reading to Mr. Bunny.

Cool. And it's not even noon yet.

Proud he had completed the assignment with time to spare, he quickly toggled over to World of Warcraft and was soon on a mission to go back to Kalimdor for a final showdown, dethroning Warchief Garrosh Hellscream.

He never heard the front door open. He never heard her leave.

He looked up some time later—how long, he didn't register—and saw Amy's chair was empty. *Ten Little Rabbits* was on the chair, opened. But no Mr. Bunny. And no Emily.

Maybe she just went to the bathroom.

He headed to the downstairs bathroom. No, not there.

"Em? Emily" Tommy peeked into the kitchen. Their breakfast dishes were still on the counter. Amy's craft project lay scattered on the island. He felt a moment's irritation about the silver glitter and art supplies all about but quickly let it go.

No Emily.

He trotted up the stairs then, his movements quicker, a sense of unease in his head. Was she napping back in her bed? He zipped into her room. The air conditioner was still running, but he could see right away that her bed was empty. "Em? Answer me!" Tommy even tugged open her closet doors; maybe she was playing hide and seek.

No Emily.

Running now, he checked their bedroom, their bathroom, the hall closet. Nothing. His heartbeat ratcheted up as unease turned to alarm.

Dashing to the back door, he searched the enclosed deck. He let the back door slam behind him—he'd been meaning to fix the hinge but hadn't found the time—and it shuddered in its frame. "Em? Emily, where are you?" He stepped off the deck, even bending to peer behind the loose lattice section next to the stairs. No Emily.

He stood in the backyard, puzzled. Where on earth—
And then he heard the screeching of tires.
A car horn, then a woman's scream.

* * * *

Sitting there in the emergency room waiting room, Tommy held her small jacket. He barely heard Amy over his own internal torment.

Why did she put her jacket on? What made her leave? Where was she going? Why didn't she pull on my sleeve like she always does? Oh God, why did I take my eyes off her?

It was all such a blur. He heard again the woman's scream, a horn, tires screeching, a dog barking, and an ambulance. The order would never be clear, but the vision of Emily lying still on the road seared into his mind. She looked so peaceful lying there. For a brief moment, he thought she was asleep. Her little bare feet turned downward, one cheek pressed to the pavement. Her body still, her face calm, and her right hand still holding on to Mr. Bunny.

Why didn't she get my attention? Why didn't I hear her? Why didn't she put her sandals on? She had been so proud of being a big girl and putting her sandals on. It's the end of June. It was ninety degrees today. Why did she take her coat?

"Tommy!"

His head snapped up, and he saw Amy glare at him briefly before she resumed talking with a young doctor not much older than Tommy. Tommy sprung to his feet.

"How is she?" Tommy blurted.

The doctor gazed at him with gentle eyes. "As I told your wife, I'm not her surgeon. Dr. Mendoza is. I'm Dr. Rohn, chief pediatric resident. Emily is still in the operating room. I just came out to give you an update." The young doctor's voice was unruffled.

"And?" Tommy insisted.

"And she has a mild concussion, multiple contusions on her left side, her left leg is broken, and she has two cracked ribs. Right now we are concerned that one of the ribs has punctured the inferior lobe in her right lung, but it's too soon to tell."

"Will she be okay?" Tommy asked, not realizing he was handing Emily's coat to the doctor.

The young doctor glanced down at the pink and green jacket with a puzzled expression and then back at Tommy. Ignoring the motion, Rohn directed his attention toward Amy and answered, "I don't know. I'll be back as soon as I know more."

Dr. Rohn gave a quick nod of concern and left the room.

For the next hour, Amy paced the waiting room, thumbed through dog-eared, outdated magazines from the tables, and bought two cans of Pepsi from the vending machine near the door. Finally, a nurse came into the waiting room. "Waal family?"

Both Amy and Tommy jumped to their feet. Amy grasped Tommy's hand tightly and briefly closed her eyes.

The nurse gave them a comforting smile. "Emily is out of the OR and is in the recovery room. Dr. Mendoza is with her. She's in good hands. You'll be able to see her shortly."

"When is that? Is she all right?" Amy asked.

"She's been admitted to the third-floor pediatrics unit, and once she's got the 'all clear' in recovery, she'll be brought up to her room. I'd estimate it will be about forty-five minutes to an hour from now." The nurse gazed at them, her expressions gentle. "While we wait for the doctor, why don't we bring Emily's things up to her room before you go see her, okay?"

They nodded numbly. Tommy questioned, "But she'll be okay? Right?"

"She's in good hands, Mr. Waal. We'll know more after she wakes up."

The nurse waited for Tommy and Amy to gather Emily's personal belongings, including Mr. Bunny, who had fallen out of Amy's purse. Tommy picked up their half-full cans of Pepsi and tossed them in the trash.

The hospital seemed like a maze to Tommy; each hallway they walked down looked identical to the one before. The fluorescent lights above were bright, and the beige, speckled floors were spotlessly cleaned. The steel railings that lined the halls looked like bumper guards. He heard echoes from every sound made, whether it was a conversation between doctors as they walked, or squeaky wheelchairs being pushed, or the screeching sound of a locked gurney being shoved up against the steel bumpers, the sounds echoed in Tommy's ears. Each person they passed seemed to know where they were going and didn't seem to be in any hurry to get there. Even their nurse escort seemed calm and relaxed. She said a hello here and there and walked as if she had all the time in the world.

Didn't she know the urgency? Didn't she know their world had just fallen apart?

In the elevator, the nurse pressed 3 for the third floor and finally turned to address them directly. "Her room is right next to the showers if either of you need to freshen up before I take you back down to recovery."

The elevator doors opened, and Tommy noticed the difference of the third floor immediately. The colorful patchwork-squared carpet smelled new. A bald, middle-aged man dressed in a black security uniform sat behind a small security table to the right of the elevator, drinking coffee. As Tommy walked past the security table, he admired the hallway walls; they had cheerful murals on them—children playing with dogs and cats; the sun shining on a beach; a happy-looking house with a family in the yard.

They passed the nurses' station where Tommy heard two nurses chatting about what they should order for lunch—shrimp and broccoli from Main Moon or calzones from Luigi's? There was that same fluorescent lighting throughout the floor, but he noticed that all the walls were again painted, these filled with children's artistic designs. One beige based wall was covered in dozens of brightly colored painted handprints with a caption "Little Hands Have Big Dreams," written in a child's handwriting.

Their friendly but efficient nurse stopped in front of a blue bin full of neatly folded white sheets and towels that smelled strongly of bleach. She smiled at the young couple as she opened the patient room's door next to it. She motioned to Tommy and Amy to walk in ahead of her.

"In here." She motioned to the room. "Emily's bed is to the left by the sink. Her roommate's bed is over by the window. She's down in x-ray right now checking on a placement from a prior surgery, but she'll be back later today."

She continued to speak as she followed behind Tommy and Amy into the room.

"Hey there, Oswin. Almost done?" The nurse smiled at the elderly janitor in the room.

"Yea-um, Miss Ellen, jus 'bout finish wit de floors," Oswin said. "It be still cold in dis here room today. Child catch a cold, de truth." He spoke softly, his head shaking back and forth as he finished mopping. He took a quick glance up at Tommy and raised his eyebrow. "Hmm, dis papa uneasy?"

Tommy just looked back at the gentleman, confused at his question. Oswin glanced over at Amy and gave a friendly nod. His attention turned back toward the job at hand, and he began to whistle.

Amy greeted the janitor with a smile and placed Emily's belongings in the small cabinet adjacent to the wrinkle-free hospital bed. Tommy glanced around. Everything looked freshly made and cleaned. The smell of lemon, pine, and ammonia was still strong. There was a small table tent sign that said: "Cleaned today—General Hospitality #701."

Amy's cell phone rang. She reached into her bag and answered it.

"Yes, Mom, she's out of surgery. We are going down to see her now. —No, she's in the recovery room now. —Yes, overnight. She's being admitted, Mom." Amy stepped over to the window and watched the sun begin to set as Tommy stood still and just looked around the room.

By the looks of it, the other hospital bed next to the window had been slept in recently. It had a blue fleece blanket crumpled at the foot of the bed, and the sterile white hospital pillowcase had been replaced with a multicolored tie-dyed one. There were at least five hand-drawn pictures that were taped to the beige walls with clear hospital tape. Some were drawn with crayons and colored pencils; others looked like they were done with the same paint colors as those on the wall of hands in the hallway. They were royal blue, vibrant green, and a few in red.

Two flower arrangements sat on the windowsill by the bed. Both were made up of blue flowers; one was filled with sprayed baby-blue carnations, and the other arrangement had a dozen blue roses and a slightly deflated "Get Well" Mylar balloon that floated above, dancing back and forth from the force of air vents. Tommy noticed two containers of chocolate pudding cups and four bags of peanut M&Ms. One of the bags had been opened. He also spotted two small piles of pennies next to a deck of playing cards and three paperback novels neatly stacked one on top of each other.

Tommy's focus turned to Amy and her conversation. "Yes, Mom, Tommy is right here." Amy glanced over at her husband. She watched him as he ran his hands through his thick, curly chestnut hair and then tugged on the scruff around his chin, as he always did when he was nervous.

He'd stopped shaving when he started taking online courses to finish his bachelor's in business management. Besides, he didn't need to shave while working at the warehouse on weekends. It paid well; he made $300 working the weekend shift while Amy worked full-time at the retail store Jams at the Galleria. He was promised full-time foreman, with benefits, as soon as he completed his degree.

They married right out of high school when they found out Amy was pregnant. They promised each other they would continue to pursue their dreams together. Since then, they'd worked around each other's job to make sure Emily didn't have to go to daycare because they just couldn't afford that. They were fortunate that Amy's grandmother had left them the house in her will last year. They could barely afford to maintain the basic necessities of being young homeowners.

Tommy let out a sigh and put his hands in his pockets as he walked past the janitor toward the window while Amy talked on the phone.

He could see the hospital's entrance and people walking in and out through the automated doors. He saw an older lady with snow-white hair in a wheelchair being wheeled out by a tall male nurse toward a black SUV. The nurse held her hand as she slowly walked toward the car. She reminded Tommy of Amy's sweet departed grandmother. His eyes scanned around and saw the large red-and-white emergency room sign only a few feet away from the entrance. An ambulance with flashing lights backed into the hospital bay behind the red-and-white sign. He could hear the ambulance's siren.

The voices were back.

Where was Emily going?

It couldn't have been for more than a second.

Why didn't she get me?

Why did she take her coat?

"Dear God, let her be okay," he whispered, both hands pressed against the window. He watched as the two EMTs jumped out of the ambulance. One opened the back door and began to pull the gurney out while the other talked to the doctor in blue scrubs. Tommy leaned closer to the window and quietly pleaded again, "Dear God, please."

He didn't hear Oswin whisper as he mopped, "Love, it be all around us, mon. It be where eyes can't see, but it hears it all. Tru dat." The janitor was done with the floor and pushed his bucket toward the hallway, resuming his whistle. He stopped his tune for a moment and stood looking out the window just as the sun began to set. He looked at the purple aster plants that were just beginning to bloom on the front lawn. His attention then turned to Tommy. "You be careful, mon. De floors be wet now." His eyes were gentle, and his teeth were whiter than Tommy had expected. As he spoke, Tommy caught the late sun's reflection on the dangling charm that hung from thick gold chain around the janitor's neck. It looked like a small bird of some sort, but he couldn't quite make it out exactly.

The janitor unfolded a yellow plastic caution sign and placed it on the floor next to Tommy's feet. When he stood back up, he had a shiny penny in his hand. "Here ya go, mon, dis must be yours." He placed the penny into Tommy's hand. "Watch on de floor next to ya, mon. Day be wet. Don't want ya mon to slip and fall."

Tommy looked at the shiny penny in his hand and began to object, "Umm … no. This isn't …"

Before Tommy could finish his protest, the door swiftly opened, and the nurse who had escorted them up reappeared. "She's awake and asking for you." She stood against the opened door to take Amy and Tommy back downstairs to the recovery room.

Amy looked up at the nurse and said into the phone, "Mom, I've got to go. They're taking us to see Emily. —Yes, we have a room. —No, no, I don't know what room number. Mom, I've got to go. I'll call you as soon as I can." She hung up the phone.

Tommy walked next to Amy. "Where'd he go?" he asked her, still holding the penny in his hand.

"Who?"

"The … ah, never mind." Tommy sighed, baffled as he looked down at the penny. He held the door as Amy followed the nurse down the hallway. Just before he walked out of the room, Tommy closed his eyes for a brief second and tossed the penny toward the other bed that was by the window. He made a quick wish as if he were making a wish at a fountain.

"Please, dear God, make this right."

The door closed behind him.

* * * *

Even in this place, you can wish, you can plead, or you can pray to God in any form you choose. Whether you know it or not, someone always hears you. You can be sure of it.

6 Pennies Are Love from Above

By the time Tommy and Amy made it back to room 313, dinner had been served. A brown cafeteria tray had been placed on the counter next to the sink. It seemed so foreign to Tommy to see a food tray next to gauze pads, alcohol wipe pads, and a roll of clear medical tape. It didn't seem like these worlds belonged together, food and medicine. Like the song on *Sesame Street* that Emily watched, it was a catchy tune; together they'd sing, "One of these is not like the other. One of these things just doesn't belong." Tommy concluded that the routine of regular life and the sterility of hospitals just didn't belong together.

Tommy could smell pizza from under the plastic-covered dish. Also on the tray was a small white Styrofoam container of vanilla ice cream that had melted through the cardboard top and a plastic-covered bowl of peach halves in a thick syrup.

The same nurse from earlier walked in the room and quickly picked up the tray. "Sorry, honey, not tonight. Tonight is strictly a frozen ice pop. Would you like cherry or grape?"

"She'll have grape, please," Amy answered and smiled down at Emily, who was quietly lying in bed. Amy half-leaned, half-sat next to her, one hand on her tiny arm.

"Grape it is." The nurse's name was Ellen according to her name lanyard badge. "I'll just get this tray out of here. We don't want to tempt her tummy until all the medicine has cleared her system and she can tolerate solid food again. I'll be right back with a grape ice pop."

Tommy sat in the wooden chair at the end of the bed. He could now hear his heart beat, steadier now, more normal. His breathing was even. The tormenting voices in his head were gone. Everything would be okay. His daughter was going to be okay.

The door opened again, and this time a woman in her thirties and a young girl, possibly twelve he guessed, walked in. Tommy assumed they were mother and daughter, based on their resemblance; both had a slim build, blonde hair, and distinctive gray-blue eyes. With her right hand, the young girl pushed a tall, metal IV pole with rubber tubing that ran between her right arm and a small, clear plastic bag that hung from its hook. The machine gave off an annoying and steady beep.

"I'm beeping!" the young girl hollered outside the door and down the hallway. "Miss Ellen, I need my flush!" she yelled. She was quite thin, Tommy noticed. With her left hand, she pulled a small green oxygen canister behind her.

The young girl turned her attention toward Emily, who was now sitting up in bed, her eyes a bit wide, and said, "Hey there, roomie. I'm Jenna. Whatcha in here for?"

Emily blushed as she looked up at her new roommate and waved Mr. Bunny in her direction. Emily oscillated her attention between the IV pole, the green canister, and the rubber tubing that rested under Jenna's nose and hung around her ears.

Jenna looked at the stuffed animal in Emily's hand. "Cute bunny. Does it have a name?" Jenna said, taking a step closer to Emily, who was quickly trying to hide her face behind Amy's arm.

"Now, Emily, don't be shy. Say hello to Jenna," Amy coaxed her daughter.

Emily's face turned red, and she just shook her head back and forth behind Amy's arm.

"Nah, that's okay," Jenna said. "I get it. First time in, first time scared."

Amy looked curiously at Jenna and then over to her mother, who was now extending her hand out to Amy.

"Hi, I'm Mary, and you've already met my very outgoing daughter, Jenna."

"Hey, look! A new penny!" Jenna exclaimed as she pushed the beeping IV pole toward her bed, dragging the canister behind. She let go of the IV pole and picked up the penny from her bed. She held the penny to the light, examining the date. "Two thousand twelve! Cool!"

"Did you win all that dough?" Tommy asked Jenna, looking over at the pile of pennies.

"These pennies? Ha! No." Jenna giggled and then pointed toward the bags of peanut M&Ms. "This here's my dough!" She looked back at Tommy. "You like to play any games, Mister?"

Tommy felt like he had been punched in the gut. "Ah … um … not cards, no," he stuttered.

The sounds were back in his head—the car horns, the screeching tires, the siren from the ambulance. They were deafening. He shook his head trying to erase the sounds.

"Well, I'll teach you then," Jenna said, interrupting his torment. "Rummy's a great game. I beat my mom all the time!" Jenna grabbed a handful of peanut M&Ms from her winnings and tossed them into her mouth.

Nurse Ellen walked in carrying a small, clear plastic

syringe filled halfway with saline, a few squares of alcohol wipes, and a grape ice pop. She handed the ice pop to Emily, whose eyes lit up.

She walked toward Jenna. "Flush time and you're free until 9:00 p.m., little lady."

"Free at last." Jenna chuckled. She detached the long rubber tubing from the green canister and twisted it to a green spout that was attached to the wall. She turned a small knob next to the spout to 3. She plopped herself on the bed and pulled the hospital tray toward her and started shuffling the cards. "So, who wants to give me their peanut M&Ms?"

"Jenna, maybe these folks want to settle in a bit. Let's not overwhelm them in the first five minutes." Mary's tone was stern.

Tommy watched Jenna in bewilderment as she got situated and then glanced over at Emily, whose lips were now tinged purple. He could see a quickly melting ice pop dripping down her little hand. Amy's face looked relaxed, and she grinned as she tried to catch the drips with her Handi-wipe. Tommy caught Amy's eyes, and they both exchanged a quick glance of relief and smiled.

"No, that's quite all right." Tommy smiled and looked over at Jenna. "You know what? I'll be right back."

Before he could get out the door, Emily whispered, "Daddy, come here," her little finger calling him closer.

Tommy leaned in to Emily's sticky face so she could whisper in his ear. "What is it, sweetheart?" he asked.

"Daddy, I need my coat now. It's cold in this room."

Tommy didn't move. He froze there, still leaning over Emily with his ear so close to her mouth he could feel her cool breath in his ear and smell the grape on her lips. His heart stopped for a moment. She needed her coat? Now?

His mind raced back to earlier, when she was lying facedown in the middle of the road, wearing her coat. It didn't make sense. It was such a hot June day. He stood up, tried to shake off his confusion, and then just shrugged it off.

There's no way she'd know she'd need her coat here. There's no way she'd know how cold this room would be. It's just a coincidence—that's all, he assured himself.

He decided his daughter needed her jacket just because she was eating a popsicle. He grabbed the pink and green jacket from the chair and gave it to his daughter. Emily quickly grabbed it, gave the melting popsicle to Amy, and put on the coat.

Amy gave a shrug in Tommy's direction, and he gave a confused shrug back. He looked over at Jenna and grinned. "I'll be right back. I'll be just a minute." He walked over and gave Amy a quick kiss on the lips and walked out the door.

A few minutes later, Tommy returned with three bags of peanut M&Ms from the hospital's vending machine.

"Ready!" Tommy said, holding up the bags in both hands. "C'mon, Emily. Help Daddy win some M&Ms."

Emily's lips were stained purple. With the jacket still on, she hugged her mother's arm, but her eyes apprehensively stayed on Jenna. Amy looked at Tommy and just shook her head slowly.

"You guys go ahead. We'll just watch," Amy answered as she put her arm around Emily and hugged her close.

"Suit yourself." Jenna shrugged. She looked over at Tommy, pretending to be serious. Her eyes narrowed. "Prepare to lose, Mister. I'm good at this." Jenna snickered as she dealt the cards.

"We'll see," Tommy said. He wasn't quite sure he remembered the rules for Rummy, but there was something special about Jenna that made him want get to know her a bit more. Her lighthearted nature intrigued him. He pulled his heavy wooden chair next to Jenna's bed and placed the three bags of M&Ms at the foot of her bed.

"Mom? You in?" Jenna looked over at Mary, who was searching in her purse for her phone.

"No, you go on ahead. Play this game without me. I need to call Daddy and tell him about today's x-ray results from the Mic-Key button placement."

"Suit yourself." Jenna shrugged and turned her attention back to shuffling. She dealt the cards and sat back, her legs Indian style on her bed, shoving the tie-dye pillow behind her back. Tommy noticed the tinge of blue of Jenna's lips as she readjusted the oxygen tubing around her ears.

By the fourth hand, Emily was sound asleep, and so was Amy. Mary had walked out into the hallway to finish her call to Jim so as to not disturb the new sleeping roommates and hadn't returned yet.

"Well, I'm already down one bag," Tommy said. "You *are* good at this."

Jenna wiggled her eyebrows and shuffled the deck again.

"I do it for the dough." She popped a few peanut M&Ms into her mouth.

"So if you play for M&Ms, then what are all these for?" he said, looking in the direction of the pile of pennies.

"Oh these?"

"Those are *love from above*," Jenna said matter-of-factly. "Don't you know that every penny found is sent straight from heaven? I have a bunch of angels that look out for me all the time. Every time I think really, really hard about it, a penny happens to pop up, like, just when I need it! Like yesterday when I had to get my IV changed because it blew in my vein. See?" She showed him the large purplish-blue bruise on her left forearm; it was raised and swollen to almost the size of a golf ball.

Such a large bruise on such a small arm bothered Tommy. He never had an IV or a bruise of that size and could only imagine how painful it must be. "Oh, wow ..." Tommy stated, his eyes wide.

"I hate when it does that." She lightly touched the bump on her arm. "So, I was scared to get another one 'cause they miss all the time and have to stick me like three or four times, and I can't move a muscle or they'll miss again." For a moment, her mouth turned downward, and she let out a little sigh. She paused as if remembering an unpleasant memory and then quickly recaptured her bubbly voice.

"And so right before they brought me to that icky room where they keep all those needles and where they put the IVs in, I saw this one!" She grabbed the penny that was next to her blue Gatorade and held it up to show Tommy. "There it was, right there on the floor! A 2013 penny! Thirteen is my lucky number! My love from above! And then I knew everything was going to be just fine." She let out a cough that sounded more like she was clearing her throat. Then she took a sip of her blue sports drink. He surmised her blue lips were due to the blue Gatorade, but he wasn't sure.

"And you know what?" she said without missing a beat. "What?"

"It was!" she said with such delight. "Miss Mia made it in with just *one* stick! That never happens!" Jenna showed Tommy her right arm where Nurse Ellen had just disconnected her from the beeping IV pole. Her right arm showed a small catheter that was threaded into Jenna's vein. It was covered with white gauze and a piece of large, clear Tegaderm tape to protect the line.

"That's great," Tommy said, searching her face, trying

to understand why someone so young could possibly be so happy in a hospital. She too was one of those things that just didn't belong here.

"That new penny on your bed was on the floor earlier, but no one was here. I guess it must have fallen from your pile," Tommy said, trying to explain her newfound penny.

"Oh, that's not my penny, Mister," Jenna said immediately.

"Really? How do you know? And please, call me Tommy," he said as he looked at the large pile of pennies on her tray.

"Because, Mr. Tommy, I know." She giggled at her new friend and continued, "See? That new one is really super shiny, and I only brought twelve special pennies with me from home, and I only found three here so far. So this 2012 love-from-above penny must be for you." She handed the shiny penny back to Tommy.

He took it and looked carefully at the date. "Hmm, 2012, huh?" he said. "Love from above, is it?" he asked Jenna.

"You betcha, Mr. Tommy. Sure is. Someone upstairs has your back." She motioned her thumb up to the ceiling.

He let out a chuckle and placed the penny next to the rest of his M&Ms. "Well, how can I argue with that," he said, unsure of what to make of his new young friend.

They finished playing Rummy, and Tommy was happy to lose his other two bags of peanut M&Ms to his new card partner.

It was 9:00 p.m. when Nurse Ellen came back in with more syringes, alcohol wipes, and two filled plastic pouches. "I've got your Tobramycin," she said.

Nurse Ellen hooked Jenna back up to the machine attached to the steel pole. She expertly punctured the antibiotic plastic pouch with the needleless end of the rubber tubing. The medicine quickly flowed through the clear rubber tubing, but before it ran out the other end, she had already threaded the plastic line through the machine and clamped it shut. She then pressed a bunch of buttons, and the machine beeped with each press of her finger. When she was done, the sound of a wheel turning inside the machine was all the noise that remained.

"Okay, sweetheart," Nurse Ellen said to Jenna. "This will run for about an hour. Then your Ceftazidime is up right after that. I'm done for the day after this, so Miss Sara is here tonight. She'll be in shortly."

Jenna's eye lit up. "Yay! I hope she brought her sweater!"

"Well of course she did, silly. She knows you're still here." Ellen smiled back at Jenna. They obviously knew each other well.

Ellen then wheeled another machine over to Emily. Emily's eyes widened with fear. "This machine just takes vitals," she explained to Tommy. "Blood pressure, oxygen concentration, and heart rate. No needles, I promise," she said to Emily. Emily's eyes didn't leave the machine, but she allowed Nurse Ellen to wrap the small blue cuff around her leg. "See?" Nurse Ellen said as she smiled at Emily. "No needles, just as I promised." After she finished taking Emily's vitals and her temperature, she put on the pink stethoscope that was hanging around her neck. She listened intently to Emily's lungs and looked over at Amy.

"She sounds really good." She seemed pleased. "Dr. Mendoza wants to keep her here tonight just for observation. After rounds tomorrow, either she or Dr. Rohn will let you know when you can go home. I'm so glad her lung wasn't punctured."

"We are too," Amy said quietly.

Ellen continued, "Okay, I'll let you have some rest until the next shift comes through." She opened the door to leave and then stopped abruptly. She turned her head back toward

Amy. "Oh, Mrs. Waal, I can't read the doctor's writing on this report, and I want to get ahead of the discharge papers. When was Emily was born?"

Amy casually responded, "February 12."

Tommy froze for a moment. He glanced quickly up at the ceiling and shook his head in bewilderment. He smiled at Jenna, then turned his head toward the nurse and said, "February 12, 2012."

* * * *

Sometimes you just can't explain it. Sometime you just know. Sometimes a penny is more than just a penny. Sometimes it's all the sense you need.

7 *Helicopters*

*T*he thunderous sound of a helicopter approaching invaded the room. It was now the first of July as Jenna looked out the window of room 313 and saw the MedEvac chopper landing on the roof above the emergency room section of the hospital. Its long blades spun above the belly of the helicopter as it lowered toward the rooftop. Its silhouette was black, like an insect set against the sky and the setting sun.

*   *   *   *

It happens here so often, the landing of the helicopter. Lives on the brink of death, their one last hope is this hospital, "the hospital of choice by all medical standards." The emergent ones have doctors rushing out to meet them on the rooftop, while others have bought enough time that they can make it downstairs into the emergency room rushed in on gurneys.

The sounds of the helicopter whirling round and round still give me a shudder every time. Even after thirty years here at General, it's something I can't get used to.

Sometimes what you see here, even decades ago, can haunt you forever …

*　*　*　*

It was 1985, a cold and blistery December evening during our first winter here at General, our first busy season. I had just relocated back to New York after ten years of working at Key West Memorial Hospital.

Yes, hospitals too have a busy season. Retailers are busiest from Black Friday until the end of the year, buying, selling, and waiting in long lines. Same here at General. Sometimes I wonder if we're not retailers ourselves. The rush, the long lines, the returns—the exchanges.

The ones who await organ transplants pray. Some have waited years for another chance to live, while some wait only days. While they wait, they pray. They pray that their lives will be saved by an unfortunate soul who is just about to lose theirs.

The *exchange*.

One life for another. Finding the perfect size and shape, perfect match, and perfect fit for the exchange. One man's hell is another man's heaven. One man's last breath is another man's first chance at a new life. Who are we to judge? We are merely the surgeons, the skilled exchangers.

While some families are in gut-wrenching sobs, saying their last good-byes, in deep, pleading prayer for that last chance, that last long shot of a hopeful miracle to save their loved one, there is a gentle-toned doctor in another room asking if their son, daughter, or parent who's barely hanging on is an organ donor. Customer service at its best.

It's all tragic, no matter how you look at it. Inevitable? No. Vultures? Perhaps. When faced with the reality of real life-and-death options, we *are* the lifesavers. Vultures to some, saviors to others.

December is always the busiest month. Time is of the essence. We sleep in shifts, we work all night, and we live under the glow of fluorescent light. Time, it's everyone's most valuable commodity, yet it's what most people take for granted. Here at General, we know we have to get emergency patients in as quickly as possible, and get them out even faster. There's a long waiting line, and the demand is high. Time is the enemy that no one pays attention to, until it starts running out.

Here in New York, the added elements of ice and snow that Mother Nature provides can increase the speed at which the doors revolve. Jack Frost complements the haste with his little touch of sleet and black ice. It's not my doing; it's just my busy season, and that's where I thrive.

I'm the store manager, the chief of this place—this hospital of choice by all medical standards—and I'm damn good at what I do.

One particular December evening in 1985—Friday, December 20, in fact—the sounds of an approaching helicopter were upon us. I remember, as I stood waiting on the rooftop, I noticed the deep orange glow of the sun setting behind the snow-covered weeping willow tree. Jack Frost had added his crystal touch, covering the trees, the grounds, and the highways. The ice reflecting the amber glow produced such a beautiful sight. I stood there fixated for a moment, not feeling the bite of cold air against my face as the chopper landed. There had been a brutal four-car accident out on Interstate 95. EMTs reported two fatalities at the scene, three victims could go by ambulance to the local hospital, and the two critical victims were flown here.

I was the hospital chief at that time. I was on top of my game. I call them the arrogant years. I had saved countless lives, and my protégé, Gray, was glued to my side. "Learn. Take notes," I'd tell him. "Watch first and then ask," I'd instruct him. And boy did he.

He reminded me of myself when I was a third-year intern. Hungry to learn with just that hint of compassion. Truth be told, he had more compassion than what was good for him. That would change in time, I thought. He was young. Time weathers everyone. Life in a hospital would certainly weather Gray.

The helicopter arrived with a husband and wife in their mid to late thirties. It had taken the firemen over two hours to pry them out of the car with the Jaws of Life. The black Mercedes sedan they were driving was crushed by the impact from the pickup truck behind them and smashed their car against the guardrail.

"Possible internal bleeding," I was told by the dispatch. The husband had been pinned to the driver's window frame by the steering wheel. The wife had head trauma and possible internal bleeding due to the direct impact of hitting the dashboard. Glass shards and blood were everywhere.

The stat team in the MedEvac chopper said they would arrived on the rooftop at 5:21 p.m. Gray and I ran out at 5:20 p.m. and watched them land.

On the helipad of the hospital, Gray assessed the wife while I ran toward the more severe case, the husband. "Sir, I'm Dr. Morgan. You've been in a serious car accident, and I need to take a look."

His face was bloody, shards of glass still embedded in his skin, and he was barely conscious. His moans were growing faint. I ran with his gurney toward the helipad's rooftop elevator while the flight team updated me with his details.

"Male, approximate age late thirties, initial heart rate 129 bpm, blood pressure 82/49, respiratory rate 34 bm. Oxygen saturation is at 87 percent. He was wearing a seatbelt during the collision. The airbag malfunctioned. A peripheral intravenous line was placed during flight on his left arm." A female doctor in a red flight suit jogged next to me, holding the gurney.

Upon quick examination, I saw that his oropharynx was clear, but his airway was patent, and his trachea appeared to be shifted to the right of midline. I bent over with my stethoscope. I heard decreased breath sounds over the left side of his chest. His carotid pulse was weakly palpable, and his jugular venous pulse was elevated.

He coded before we could get him to the operating room.

I took measures to keep his heart pumping while we rode the elevator down to the main floor.

"Hang on, we're almost there," I said to the husband as his eyes rolled back into his head. "Stay with me!"

I continued with chest compressions the entire way down the hallway, giving him an intracardiac shot of adrenaline to the heart. Rushing down the hall with me, Nurse Jackie took out the newly acquired portable automated external defibrillator.

Still racing down the hallway, I yelled, "Clear!" as the defibrillator shocked him.

He didn't respond. I continued giving him rapid chest compressions, but his pulse never elevated.

We never made it inside the operating room, and I pronounced John Doe dead at 5:47 p.m. on December 20, 1985 in the hallway right outside my OR.

I took off my rubber gloves and threw them in the red bin just outside the double doors.

Shit! I hate losing. I was so close. Shit!

I looked inside my operating room, still sterile, unutilized. My frustration grew.

Now I have to tell his wife.

I hated this part. The one who has to inform the next of kin. Especially a spouse. *Shit. If I could have just gotten him into the OR, I could have saved him. I know I could.*

I hate losing.

I had to tell her, since I was the one who called his time. I was the one who had to inform the next of kin. It would take me all of ten minutes.

I'd done it enough times to know you get straight to the point. You give them all the facts, you look directly into their eyes, and you tell them quickly with little emotion—and never forget to show just a hint of compassion. You let them ask, you let them cry, you let them swear at you for not doing more. I was ready.

I walked swiftly down the hallway to get the conversation behind me when my pager went off. "Code blue."

"Code blue, Trauma Unit 4," the PA system blared. "Dr. Morgan, code blue, Trauma Unit 4," it repeated, my pager vibrating again.

The wife—she was crashing.

Shit!

I quickly approached the unit. I could see she was in ventricular tachycardia and quickly losing consciousness.

"Alex, she's going into shock," Gray informed me.

I grabbed another pair of rubber gloves from the wall container and rushed next to him.

I looked up at the monitor and could see her numbers were critical. Her blood pressure was quickly dropping, and her heart rate was at 170. Gray gave her chest compressions, and I quickly jumped in to relieve him. While looking up at the monitor, I called out for 150 mg of Amiodarone. I quickly placed the heel of my hand on the center her chest. I pushed hard and fast.

"Ma'am, I'm Dr. Morgan, and I—" I looked down at the wife. I froze.

She was still conscious but barely. Through her bloodstained face, she was able to look up at me. Our eyes connected, both in disbelief.

It can't be. I stared at her face, her lips, and her eyes.

It can't be.

Locked in a gaze, time froze for a mere second. I was unable to take my eyes off her, and my memory started to wander. Alarms blared once more. Her eyes rolled into the back of her head, and blood began trickling out of her mouth.

"Alex!" Gray shouted at me.

Immediately, I was back in action, and she became just another Jane Doe I needed to save. By all accounts, she was coding. Gray and I continued to take turns giving her chest compressions in efforts to stabilize her.

Jackie, the ICU nurse, took over the ordeal of connecting her to all the IVs to put her in a medically induced coma, to relieve her body of the stress while we tried to save her.

It took Gray and me over thirty minutes to get her stabilized, but she was alive, unconscious, and in critical condition.

"What the hell was that, Alex?" His glare was angry, and his face flushed. "Where the hell were you a minute ago?"

"She's stable now. I'll update her chart, and I'll be back." I ignored his question.

"No, Alex," he said with authority. "I'll take care of that." He huffed. "I don't know where the hell you were or what the hell just happened, but you had better get your act together before you step foot back in here." He left the room.

It was her.

She was alive.

It was Vivian.

She was still as beautiful as I had remembered.

8   *Escape to Paradise*

Key West, 1975

*A*s a doctor, I had been a shooting star. Medical school at Cornell University was a breeze, and when I graduated, I did my internship at New York-Columbia Medical Center. There I flew through the ranks during my residency, and by age twenty-five, I was Dr. Alex Morgan, chief surgical resident. I was young and arrogant and wanted it all. I was a workaholic who loved my job. Hell, I excelled at my job. I'd work sixteen-hour days every day of the week. A 115-hour workweek was normal. It was mandatory hospital policy to take twenty-four hours off every six days, but I never followed rules. I wouldn't log in, but I'd be there. Eat, sleep, and play there. Hospitals were my home and my playground. I was needed almost every minute of every day; nothing gave me a higher rush. I could fix any patient that came through my operating doors. Anyone who wasn't a patient, I had no use for. I never did play well with others in the real world because relationships had too many needy obligations, so many issues, and I had zero interest in trying to fix them, not without anesthesia anyway.

Outside of my hospital walls, people had problems, and they needed constant attention. They had demanding emotions, required a personal relationship, and took too much of my precious time. They were never a quick fix but rather an abyss of complex sentimental weight.

As a doctor in a hospital, I could fix anything, and I never had to get attached. I gave each patient 100 percent of my undivided attention, and when they were well enough to move on, so was I. It was like speed-dating with strangers. "Name, date of birth, why are you here? Okay, great. Let me fix you and then let's go our separate ways. The only number I need is your insurance number, and please give that to the receptionist on your way out. Thank you. Please come again."

It was my life.

It was my love.

It was my obsession.

I was contemplating where I wanted to do my surgical fellowship after Columbia. Columbia had asked me to stay on and join their highly accredited surgical unit. They sweetened the deal with the promise of attending chief in three years. I didn't want a private practice; that just meant close relationships—with staff, with nurses, with patients— and I wanted none of that. Hospitals, emergency room, and daily impersonal chaos, now *that* was my calling.

I had no family, no real home to speak of, and I had just spent seven years of my life buried in Columbia. It was then that something inside of me started to yearn for a change of scenery. I loved the hospital, but when my day was done at Columbia, I had no outlet, no place to relieve the stress of hospital life. I wanted somewhere far, far away from New York. Far away from school, far from my foster family, far away from my past and anyone who knew me.

I wanted contrast.

By day, I worked in rubber soles under fluorescent

lighting, and by night I yearned for the natural glow of a tropical sunset. Concrete and sand. Hospital air and Mother Nature's warm, salty breeze. Good-looking on the outside, ugly in. I was built for contrast. I was built for all or nothing.

Hospitals were like Vegas for me. I never knew what the weather was like outside, and I didn't care. I didn't know if it was night or day, and I didn't care. My world thrived inside four operating walls, and I was all in.

The pulse of an emergency room was my drug of choice, the chaos coursing through my veins. Each crisis was a hit that fed my addiction. Being a doctor kept me numb from being human. I was addicted to the sterile smell. I got a rush from lives on the brink of death. I was never higher than when I was in demand and in need. The irony was I had great social skills in a hospital, as a doctor. I had horrible intimate skills and was unable to have close friends or relationships in person, as a man.

In a hospital, I was admired for my skill, my gift, my ability to save lives.

I'm sure my condition didn't seem obvious to others, but my disorder, if you will, prevented me from having any sort of long-term relationship, friend or lover. A psychologist might have said it was to compensate for being placed in three different foster families, or excelling so well in school that when I graduated at the age of sixteen, Mr. O'Brien, my biology teacher, was my only friend. Either way, I was a freak. My social worker called me "unique." The school guidance counselor said I had "great potential," but the kids at school knew better. Kids see right through to the real you. I was *Alex the Freak* to them, and it fit. They weren't being mean; at least I didn't take it that way. They just put to words what I already knew. You can't break the broken.

Hospitals were my sanctuary. The emergency room protected my anonymity. I never saw the faces after the post-op visit. Don't get me wrong: just because I didn't care about people's feelings long-term, that didn't mean I wasn't a master at my job. Ask any of my patients, and they'd tell you I have a very charming bedside manner with a delightful hint of compassion. I just never got too attached to anyone. That wasn't part of the job or in the Hippocratic oath. I was made to save people, and I would never acknowledge that deep down I was the one who needed saving.

Perhaps moving south was deliberate, but I doubt it. I don't recall actually thinking it through. My ego would never let me compromise my quality of work even though my heart was growing colder. I'm assuming it was my subconscious that finally took over. When it became easier to decide between a #12 crescent-shaped blade or a #15 downward-angle scalpel to slice open another John Doe's chest cavity than deciding if I wanted milk or sugar in my coffee, I knew it was time for a change. It was time for contrast. The notion of watching the sun melt into the horizon and witnessing it disappear into the nothingness gave me the possibility that, just maybe, I could replenish my soul with a promise that come sunrise, I'd have another chance to get it right.

After a life in New York with its fast pace and its cold winters that slowly occupied my soul, I grabbed the first available job offer that was as far south as I could go. I had an impressive and notable job offer at Key West Memorial Hospital on 1010 Windsor Lane. It sounded about as opposite from New York as I could possibly get.

Key West, Florida, filled with stories of poverty and prosperity, death and rebirth, became my home. Key West Memorial Hospital became my refuge. It was a fairly new hospital, built in 1971, and it was the area's only hospital south of the Seven Mile Bridge that provided health care to the conchs, fresh waters and otherwise.

In Key West, the residents call themselves "conchs." Saltwaters were born here, and the Freshwaters lived in Key West for at least seven years. I stayed down long enough to be called Freshy.

When I arrived in June 1975, I answered a "Charming 2-bedroom Key West Hospitality at 701" rental ad in the *Key West Citizen* classifieds and rented a room in a small, two-bedroom house on 701 Pauline Street, just a half mile from Key West Memorial. The pier was only a mile away, and I could walk everywhere I needed to go.

My roommate, Oz, and I got along great. I appreciated how he kept to himself and didn't invade my privacy much. He traveled often, I suppose. It was that or I just didn't notice him around the small cottage. On a few occasions when our schedules crossed, we'd walk down Duval Street, and he'd stop for a cigar, chat with a few of his friends, and then we'd grab dinner at Seven Fish. He was a few years older than I was, and folks in town called him Wizard of Oz or the Dred of Oz. I never asked him what he did, and he never asked me. We're all freaks down here in the Keys—me in my scrubs and he in his Rasta tam.

I did my surgical fellowship at Key West Memorial and stayed on to become an attending doctor. By my second year, I was chief of surgery for their ER. I was the young genius doc everyone was talking about that could shorten the surgical time by fifteen minutes using a stitch method that naturally seemed to make more sense than what I had been shown at Columbia. Between that and having no fear, no family, and a steady hand, I quickly had job offers around the country. But at that point in my life, the Keys was where I felt most at home. I was a loner, and I was happy.

My days were spent operating on patients inside the hospital—precise, driven, focused. My evenings were spent watching the sunset celebration down at Mallory Pier, admiring the tourists, and taking full advantage of the ample supply of the revolving one-night stands. The satisfied, one-night outpatients willingly welcomed my master surgical hands in the dark—precise, driven and focused. I'd leave before daylight broke, the mysterious, seductive doctor they could tell their friends about when they returned home as I returned to mine. My home, Key West Memorial. I was married to my job, and to her I was committed. I had it all. We understood one another; we connected. She was my beating sustenance. She fed me, and I adored her magnificence.

Down in the Keys, Wednesday was my day off. I began to look forward to the break from work, even if it was for only a day. On Wednesdays, I'd hang with the sunset crowd down on Mallory Square. I walked just west of the northern end of Duval Street, surrounded by fellow gypsies and freaks; it was the perfect way to be alone. I'd follow the legend that Tennessee Williams initiated of applauding the sunset; though he had a gin and tonic in hand, I chose tequila. I appreciated his tradition of giving glory to the auburn sun setting off in the distance. I'd toast the splendor in the sky with my tequila, club soda, and a twist of lime.

My fellow freaks and I were in search of our own personal paradise. They were often high on LSD, and I was coming down from the high of my run at the hospital. All of us freaks believed that we could watch the mythical Atlantis rise from the cloud formations at sunset, looking out into the horizon. The skies glowed with blues, purples, pinks, and golds every night, like magic.

Every sunset seemed to promise a new day, a new beginning, a melting of a cold heart. Every sunset, I'd gaze deep into the deep turquoise water, wondering, contemplating—could I survive?

I became very fond of the myth of the mystical Atlantis. The myth that Atlantis eventually fell out of favor with the gods and submerged into the Atlantic, that it that sank under the weight of its own perfection.

9 *Coral Reefs and Sunsets*

Wednesday, May 18, 1977

*J*immy Buffet had just released his latest album, *Changes in Attitude and Changes in Latitude,* and that summer he was frequently spotted drunk and singing one of his new hits in a local bar off Duval Street. The crowds came for Jimmy, sunsets, and the newly famous margaritas. The old LSD freaks with their gin and tonics were being replaced with a guitar-strumming wanderer in flip-flops, holding a tequila drink made in paradise. Buffet's influence expanded quickly. Tourists of all kinds—wayward dreamers and an influx of cruise ships—began to stream into the Keys. Souvenir shops, street performers, and homeless panhandlers grew in numbers as Key West became a hot tourist attraction. The magicians, psychics, and local artists all captivated the tourists' attention and wallet.

It was Wednesday, my day off, and the only day of the week I wasn't even on call. It was all mine to be alone in my thoughts. I took my usual walk up Elizabeth Street to Greene Street just past Duval and stopped in my standard watering hole, Captain Tony's Saloon, for a few shots of tequila with lime. Then I'd stroll down streets lined with palm trees and keepsake shops to the pier before sunset to watch the magical nightly performance and assess the latest influx of female tourists.

The night air was perfect, and Mallory Square was packed. There were musicians—guitar players with tambourines strapped to their legs and saxophone players, acoustic jazzy melodies—along with street performers of all kinds and artists selling their art. There were couples holding hands lost in the romantic trance of the cotton-candy sky. My gaze eventually caught three young college girls giggling as they sat on the stone wall, sipping their drinks, waiting on the sunset.

The scene could have been a lyric out of a Jimmy Buffet song. I was fascinated by her instantly. She was sitting there, her long blonde hair pulled back in a ponytail, yellow sundress, and a laugh that caught my attention immediately. Her whole face lit up when she laughed. I couldn't help but stare as I watched her in deep conversation with her friends. I decided to grab a seat at El Meson, the closest outside bar to her and the sunset, and ordered a tequila with club soda and lime.

The warm orange blaze of the sun was just beginning to vanish into the Gulf of Mexico. I stood up and turned to view the entertainment before me. I made idle chitchat with my drinking neighbor about the invasion of so many tourists, but my eyes were focused solely on her.

She caught my stare and waved me over.

"Hey, you, there!" she called. "Don't just stand there gawking. Please do us a favor and take our picture with the sunset?"

I smiled, caught in the act of admiration. I left my drink and walked over to where they were. As she handed me her camera, I let our hands briefly touch. Then our eyes connected longer than she apparently felt comfortable. She quickly dropped her gaze.

With her eyes looking down at the camera, she said, "So, please be a dear and get a good picture of us?" She glanced back up at me. "Okay?" With her other hand, she pointed to the rustic stone wall behind them. "Let's stand here, girls." They hustled next to her and adjusted their dresses. The redhead ran her fingers through her curls, springing them looser around her shoulders.

"Sure thing," I said, raising the camera to take their picture.

"And quickly please. The sun is setting," she urged as she turned her attention toward the horizon. The sun and sky, the greatest of all street performers, showcased their dance in dramatic, graceful hues of auburn, red, and orange.

The three girls lined up side by side against the wall, holding their drinks up in the air.

"Cheese!" they said in unison.

"On no, dear ladies," I interjected, lowering the camera to my waist. "We must capture the authenticity of such an event, right?"

The brunette arched her back, put her hand on her thick waist, and gave a puzzled look. The blonde just looked at me. I could tell I piqued her curiosity.

"You see, my dear ladies, down here we don't say *cheese*." I shook my head, looking directly into the eyes that captured me from afar. "Oh no. Down here in the Keys, we say, 'See you at sunset.'" My smile widened as I drew the camera back to my face.

My eyes focused on hers, her gaze now capturing my heart like a thief.

They all stood back in line, raised their drinks, and repeated, "See you at sunset. *Cheeeeese!*" Then they giggled, titillating and girlish, full of energy, hope, and youth.

I took a few pictures of them by the stone wall and then a few more of just her. The glow of the setting sun outlined her body like a priceless painting. I returned the camera to her freckled-face redheaded friend and directed my question specifically to the blonde. "So what brings you ladies down here to the Keys?" I asked.

Her redheaded friend answered, "Oh we came down here after graduation to help Vivian settle in."

Ah, her name is Vivian.

"Yeah," added the brunette. "We're here because Vivian's sister doesn't approve of her being down here." She giggled at her inside joke.

"Yeah, well that's cause she such a prude," Red added. She looked me up and down and then asked, "You live here?" Her hazel eyes darted at me as if to question my being.

"Yes," I responded, looking directly at Vivian and giving my most flirtatious of smiles, "I do."

"Oh really?" The heavyset brunette glared. "And what exactly do you do here in the Keys? Peddle trinkets and margaritas to college grads?" she grunted.

"No," I politely answered her. "Actually I work over at Key West Memorial Hospital."

"As what?" Her eyes gave me another once over.

"As the ER chief," I answered with a grin. That line always worked like a charm.

"You're a doctor?" she gasped.

"Get out!" her freckled-faced redheaded friend exclaimed.

"Well, when I'm not peddling margaritas to college girls, that is," I joked.

"College graduates!" the heavyset brunette corrected me.

"Ah, yes—*graduates*," I repeated. "My apologies, ladies. Congratulations on such an accomplishment." I gave a slight animated bow of acknowledgment. Vivian grinned and responded with a polite nod. I knew she could feel the tension, the attraction that naturally stood there between us in the silence of the moment.

The girls just looked at each other for a minute.

"Thanks, and eh—thanks for taking our picture, Doc," said Red. I took it as an indication they were done with my picture-taking services for the evening.

"Well, have fun, ladies. Do enjoy the evening," I remarked.

"See you at sunset." I coyly smiled at Vivian.

I gave a friendly good-bye wave and headed back toward my drink.

"Hey, Doc?" Vivian called out in my direction. "What's your name?"

I stopped and slowly turned back around and gave her a smile that had more than just a hint of compassion. I replied, "Alex."

Our eyes connected, even from across the crowd, her light gray-blue eyes now etched in my mind.

"Well, Alex," she said a bit louder. "Nice to meet you." She smiled and gave me a wave that was more of a hello than a good-bye.

Addicts know these things. They know the minute they've replaced one addiction for another. I knew in that instant I had just met mine.

10 Captain Tony and His Fish

hree days later, I had just finished a thirty-six-hour
shift, and instead of going home to sleep, I took
my stroll down Duval Street. The May afternoon
air was hazy, temperatures were in the nineties, and the
humidity made it feel well over one hundred degrees. I
made a left onto Greene Street and popped into Captain
Tony's for a few tequilas and club sodas with lime before
heading down to the pier to watch the sunset.

After an hour or so, the place grew more and more
crowded as folks piled in to get out of the sweltering heat.
Lately, they'd come in to Tony's hoping to hear Jimmy Buffet
play. Jimmy used to play there often, before he became
famous. Years before Jimmy got paid in dollars to sing, Tony
would pay him in drinks and tips as Jimmy serenaded his
happy hour crowd. Jimmy started having quite a following
in this little bar on Greene Street. Captain Tony himself
loved to hear Jimmy sing and was happy to have him play
anytime he was in town. Jimmy went on to write the song
"Last Mango in Paris" in honor of his dear friend Tony.

I finished my tequila and gave my seat to a stoutly
middle-aged couple who had traveled down to Key West
from Ohio. *I'd run away too if I lived in Ohio*, I thought as I

paid my tab and offered my seat to the woman wearing an extra-large white souvenir T-shirt that read *I'm in Key West, Wish you were Beer.*

As I waved good-bye to Tony, I reached in my pocket to grab any loose change. Whatever I found in my pocket, I'd throw into the grouper's mouth before I left. Tony was a fisherman and a local charter boat captain; he probably did some kind of side business that no one talked about, and I wasn't about to ask. Throwing loose change into the grouper was a tradition here at Tony's, a tradition turned superstition that all the locals knew about.

The tale goes, many years ago Captain Tony wrestled and caught a five-foot Atlantic Goliath grouper that he proudly mounted above the door of his saloon. He loved to tell the story about how he spent four grueling hours snaring the underwater beast to anyone who'd listen. He paid homage to the mighty creature by displaying his catch above his establishment entrance. Tony claims the fish's feisty spirit lives on, and one can leave the island with good luck and blessings if you can get a coin into the mouth of the jewfish. He swears it's true. I always did it because it's what you did out of respect for Captain Tony and his tale, certainly not because I believed in superstition. I believe you make your own luck. Besides, I wasn't planning on leaving the island anytime soon, and it was a way to get rid of my loose change. I admired Captain Tony; he was a rugged, hardworking ladies' man, and though he never made it past the ninth grade, he was arguably Key West's most beloved conch.

At some point in the night, he'd always tell me, "You know what?" his breath thick of whiskey. "All you need in this life is a tremendous sex drive and a great ego. Brains don't mean shit, Doc. You know that?"

"Well." I'd smile at him. "Good thing I have all three."

He'd laugh, slap my back, and slur, "Doc, you do. You most certainly do."

Without fail, every time I left the bar, I'd toss a coin up to the damn fish and miss. I reached in my pocket and pulled out a shiny penny. I tossed it, and wouldn't you know it? In it went—in the belly of the beast. *Ha,* I thought. *Well that's a first.*

Leaving the bar, I could feel the dense air hit me. It would rain soon. There was something about humid air I really savored. It was such a contrast to the circulated hospital-grade air-conditioning I lived in at Memorial. Humidity has a way of erasing any false pretense of what you think you are and leaves you open to the elements of truth—the frizzy hair, the sweat on your brow, the flush in your skin. There's no hiding from nature's elements, and 90 percent humidity is the closest a person can get to breathing under water. Only the strong can breathe in this condition.

I took the mile walk, mostly gazing at the tourists as they ducked into a local trinket shop to cool down, or I'd watch them as they raced to eat their ice cream as it was melting down their hand. I studied the romantic couples holding hands walking down the narrow streets of Key West, oblivious to heat and their sticky clothes. Love, it seemed to be such a blinding emotion, and that thought terrified me.

The sun was beginning to set by the time I made it to Mallory Square. The light breeze from the gulf had slightly cooled the night air. People were already gathered awaiting the evening's entertainment. I fought the urge to find her, to see her just once more. I decided to just seek out another replacement, another out-of-town outpatient, a one-night stand. But my eyes scanned the crowd searching for her and no one else. Within a few minutes, my pulse quickened, and my heart started to pound. There she was. Her hair in a loose braid that rested on the bare of her back. Her flowered strapless sundress danced against her lightly tanned skin as she moved. Her laugh carried over the crowd, soothing my soul. I stood there, unable to move, afraid to lose the intoxicating high of the moment.

I watched her for a few minutes as she talked to her friends. She was engaged in conversation with her redheaded friend. I could see her right eyebrow arch as she spoke and her hands enhancing the emotion of the conversation.

It wasn't long before she, once again, caught my stare and looked in my direction. Red turned her head toward what held Vivian's attention.

"Hey look," her redheaded friend said loudly in my direction. "Doc's back."

As any good addict knows, you always hide the addiction from plain sight. You never let it show, and you never admit it. It's your secret, and if you're really in deep, you learn to hide it even from yourself.

I smiled back and waved. I took Red's comment as an invite and walked toward them. When I was just a few feet away, I said to Red, "Ladies, it's Alex, and I don't recall getting your names last we met."

"Well, Doc," Red continued, "I'm Rebecca, and this is Lily, and you took like a dozen pictures of Vivian"

"Did I now?" I smirked.

"Umm, yeah. We got those pictures developed, and half of them were just of Viv," Lily said. "Now listen, Doc," she continued, wagging her chubby finger in my direction.

"Alex," I interrupted.

"Now listen, *Doc*," she repeated. "Don't get any foolish ideas. She's not that kind of girl."

I smiled politely. "Okay, got it." I raised both my hands

in a lighthearted surrender. "I don't want any trouble here. I was just doing what I was asked."

I offered to buy them a drink, but Lily and Rebecca ran off before they could give me an answer, saying they had just spotted Jimmy Buffet or a man with bare feet singing in the marketplace.

"Oh, I just know that's him," said Lily. "I heard he plays at a local bar in town all the time." Lily grabbed Rebecca's hand, and they ran off to investigate.

"You coming, Viv?" Lily shouted back at Vivian.

"Nah, you guys go ahead. I'll save our spots," Vivian called back.

I gave her my best inviting grin. "So you're not what kind of girl exactly?" I asked.

"Oh, I know your type, Alexander. And I'm here to work." She tried to sound serious, her right eyebrow arched. "I'm spending the summer down here interning. Working," she corrected herself.

Even her eyes smiled when she talked.

"I'm here for the summer, interning—*working* at Truman Annex. We're dredging the water for coastal erosion," she said. "All these new cruise ships are compromising the coral reefs and vegetation. There's been a major disruption in the Florida Keys' sea life. The fish, lobster, and crabs have been forced to migrate elsewhere. The ecosystem is becoming a big problem." Her hands were gesturing like an exuberant child.

I couldn't help but be drawn to her. The heat and the humidity of the day exposed her natural beauty. The pink of her lips, the golden tone of her skin, the honey-colored strands of hair escaping the twist of her braid. I could feel my heart beat hard as I carefully leaned in, closer to her delicate skin, the provocative scent of her perfume. I just sat there enchanted and listened as she continued.

"And don't even get me started on the pollution that's occurring from cargo ships and oil spills. We're still recovering from the seven-million-gallon spill of the *Argo Merchant* ship in Nantucket last year. So I'm working down here all summer to do all we can to correct the mess."

"Ah, I see," I said. "All summer, you say?"

She turned her head sideways and held my gaze for a moment.

"And your friends? I asked. "Are they staying as well?"

She looked at me, questioning my inquiry. "No. They're leaving in a few days." She turned her attention to searching the crowd. After a few minutes, she looked back at me, my attention still focused on her. Her eyes quickly danced with mine, and her interest grew inquisitive. "So, Alexander, how long have you lived down here in Key West?" she asked.

"A few years now. You can't beat the Keys, really," I said, looking out over the vast turquoise water. I took a deep breath in, contemplating my next move, and chose my best-practiced one-night outpatient line. I delivered it slowly, after a long-weighted sigh. "Seems like my heart is just drawn here to the warm night sky, watching the sun slowly descend through the clouds, just waiting for it to plunge into the deep and inviting waters of the mighty gulf." I paused for that long rehearsed second and added, "After all I experience each day at Memorial, the grim things I witness, the dire people I operate on in the OR—I need this time to let everything go, to unwind—to release the pressure of it all. So, I come down here, alone, to witness all this magnificence unfold." My hands directed our attention to the sun touching the horizon off in the distance.

I was excellent at one-night stands. I could, and did, charm the panties off any woman I baited. A young good-looking doctor was easy fodder for women at any age. Hook, line— and I could mount them just like Captain Tony's grouper. It was strictly catch and release. I never kept anything I caught. But she seemed different. She just sat there and let the silence linger between us. I could see her skin glisten in the light of the setting sun. After a moment, she continued to discuss the harming impact to the coral reef as we looked out upon the horizon. Her words flowed smoothly like a calming river, and I was spellbound with every word. She captured my attention with each sentence, and her voice somehow soothed my soul. She stopped for a moment and looked out at the emerald water before us. She took a deep breath in, closed her eyes, and let the air slowly exhale past her pink, parted lips.

"There's something about a sunset to soothe the soul," she tenderly said.

My head spun as if she could read my mind. I kept quiet and let her continue. "It's the best way to end any day you're having, you know?" She looked at me. This time she didn't look away. Our eyes made contact like souls reconnecting after a lifetime apart. Her eyes so blue, searching deep into mine. It caught me off guard how she could reach in past my façade and touch my soul with just a look. Uncomfortable with the thought of exposing my vulnerability, I broke the gaze and scanned the crowd.

"I certainly do," I calmly answered. "In fact, I'm here every night that I possibly can be. Usually it's Wednesday night. The crowds are small during the week, so I have this splendid place all to myself to contemplate my day." There was the Alex the women knew and loved. I then jokingly added my personal hidden secret. "The weekend is when all the freaks come out."

"So you're here then too?" She laughed.

I looked at her and wondered, could she see right through me? No, I was certain she was just flirting. I knew that game well. Women and sunsets came easy down here in the Keys. They'd both last about the same amount of time. I had no time for romance; quite frankly, I wasn't interested. I was already married to a very demanding wife who took my energy, my hours, and my soul—Key West Memorial.

I think my arrogance is what women found so attractive. They always wanted to fix me. Ironically, I'm the one who fixes people, yet I was indisputably unfixable. Starry-eyed romance to them, outpatient service call to me, sex was a mere distraction when my primal need arose. For years, I'd stroll down here, watch the sunset, and entertain the void in my heart that my brain never acknowledged.

Catch and release. Captain Tony would be proud.

But she was different. The air around her just made it easier to breathe. She intrigued me. Her beauty surely attracted me, but her eyes, they captured my soul.

I just watched her as she spoke. Her lips parted slightly as she thought of words to finish her sentences, her face lively with expression.

She continued to talk about her internship. "We're down at the Naval Station Key West. It was just recently decommissioned in 1974—you know, down by Fort Taylor?" she asked.

"We call it Fort Zach." My instinctive need to be right got the best of me. "But please, go on," I apologized.

I didn't want her to stop talking. My God she took my breath away. I didn't say another word as she continued to talk about vertebrates, invertebrates, aquatic mammals, and marine ecosystems.

She sat there with the sunset illuminating her beauty. I've

never been more present in the sight of complete perfection. The sky's sunset recital was executed with such splendor. The cumulus clouds clung together with the most delicate of softness, slowly parting with just enough space to let the blue sky perform its wonder. The orange glow of the sun took its solo as it fell through the arrangement of the cherry and amber sky. For a moment, I pondered if Atlantis had finally risen.

It seemed like a lifetime had passed in a second when her friends came back, sweaty and giggling. "Well, it wasn't Jimmy, that's for sure, just another bum with a guitar," Rebecca said, deflated. "But I heard a rumor he's playing at some place called Captain Tony's Saloon. Some guy said it's not far from here. Want to go?"

Vivian looked at me as if she wanted to stay longer but turned to her friends. "Yes! Of course!" She looked back at me and asked, "Do you know this place?"

"I've heard of it." I smiled. "Have fun, ladies."

"Thanks, Doc," Lily said.

Vivian ran a few steps with her friends and then stopped for a moment. She paused, then turned back toward me and with a flirtatious smile said, "See you at sunset, Alexander."

She waited a moment as I responded, "See you at sunset, Vivian." I waved.

I just stood there and watched. Her dress swayed back and forth as she ran off with Lily and Rebecca. I could still hear her laugh in the distance. I took a deep breath in and held it. The scent of her perfume still lingered in the air and invaded my lungs.

11 *See You at Sunset*

*A*fter that evening with Vivian, I wasn't able to leave the hospital for days. Working four consecutive sixteen- to eighteen-hour days was nothing new for me, but now my desire to be at Memorial around the clock had diminished. When my mind wasn't focused on surgery, it was fixated on Vivian in her yellow sundress, at the pier, watching the sunset. After each long surgical shift, I thought I'd be able to take a break and stroll down to Mallory Square, but there had been a multi-casualty accident on one of the cruise ships, and all the patients were sent to Memorial. The cruise ship's plank, which connects from the ship to the dock, had come loose and sent five people into the gulf. Two had jumped, just barely missing the pier, and one person hit his head on the dock before falling into the water twelve feet below.

There had also been several incidents with the homeless vagrants that brought more of them into the ER. Sheriff Freeman had to hire more officers to his force due to the increasing use of narcotics, the influx of more vagabonds, and the frequency of drug overdoses that was growing in Key West. They all kept me busy day after day. The drifters doubled in numbers as the tourists grew. I'd get the homeless into the ER nightly; they fought constantly over squatting rights and boundaries of where they could panhandle the tourists. These shirtless, toothless addicts made being homeless their careers. Addiction knows no restrictions and hits all occupational levels.

I didn't see the light of day until late Wednesday. The sun was still out when I walked down Duval Street past Fogarty's restaurant before turning onto Greene Street for my usual tequila stop at Captain Tony's Saloon. It was still early when I headed toward Front Street. I smelled the Cuban cigars wafting in the air nightly—though I never smoked, I thoroughly enjoyed the pleasant aroma. Ernest Hemingway was noted for walking these streets with a good Cuban cigar. My housemate, Oz, knew all the cigar shops in Key West and could hand-roll a clear Havana tobacco cigar in under thirty seconds. He spent years hanging out at the Key West Havana Cigar shop on Duval and exercised his freedom to roll, smoke, and enjoy his bold-flavored tobacco. He'd tell me rolling was an art and that true aficionados never cap their cigars; they taper the ends. Oz would question why anyone would cover what's meant to be savored, saying that what is real doesn't need to be covered no matter how imperfect it appears. Oz loved his cigars, and the only Cuban cigar he'd smoke was one he rolled himself with the fresh Cuban tobacco from the fertile red soil of Viñales, a hundred miles southwest of Havana—Havana only ninety miles south of Key West. The cigar stores on Duval Street proclaimed Key West as "Cigar City, USA" and that slogan sold well to the volume of tourists wanting a taste of Cuba. Oz appreciated a good Cuban cigar, but nothing—he'd shake his head back and forth—nothing could compare to the tobacco leaves from May Pen, Jamaica sprayed with a mist of Bethune. I took another long whiff of the pungent air and crossed the street toward El Meson.

El Meson was a popular tourist spot to have drinks,

Cuban food, and watch the sunset. It's quaint atmosphere with painted walls full of flowers and art made it a highly desirable location for locals and tourists alike. I sat at the outside bar, ordered my drink, and spotted her immediately.

Vivian was sitting on the rock ledge, sipping a drink while balancing a half-eaten piece of key lime pie on her lap. Her tanned skin looked even more sun-kissed by her pastel orange blouse and white shorts, her blonde hair cascading down over her shoulders. She was engrossed in a book, and I in her. I sat there and finished my drink engaged in the view. I paid my tab and headed over to Caroline's, the new key lime pie food cart in Mallory Square, and bought myself a slice.

As I walked toward Vivian, I could see her trying to ignore the begging hands from Looting Louie. Looting Louie had been in my ER more times than I could count; he'd been stabbed, punched, and burned as a result of living on the streets. He was fairly harmless and never fought back. That probably explained all the visits to my ER. I quickened my pace and in seconds was a few feet away from Vivian.

"Hey, Louie, move along," I said to the toothless vagrant.

"I ain't doin' no wrong, Doc," he answered defensively. "I'm just asking this lovely lady to help a man down on his luck is all."

Vivian looked up at me in surprise.

"Louie, I'm telling you to move along. Now," I ordered.

The old man grumbled and walked away toward a group of tourists taking pictures by the cruise ship.

"Do you know everyone on this island?" she asked.

"Only the ones that see me often at Memorial," I answered. "He's a regular there. We call them frequent flyers."

"Oh?" she said, looking at Looting Louie, who was now

begging to a new group of tourists. Her eyes softened as if she felt sorry for the homeless man.

"Are your friends back home?" I asked, trying to take her attention away from the hobo.

"Yes. They left on Monday."

"Key lime pie?" I motioned as I held up my plate of dessert next to hers, as if it were coincidental that I was having what she was having.

"But of course," she answered. "When in Rome, right?" She held up the pie next to mine in a toast.

We bantered for a few minutes, eating our key lime pie and watching the sun set. I always marveled at how fast the sun could slip away and disappear into the horizon.

"You know," I said as the sun melted into the sea, "everywhere else in the world, the sun is merely expected to rise, shine all day, and set again. Yet here in the Keys, it's expected to perform." I motioned to the bustling crowd on the pier, all standing on the edge watching. "I mean, where else is there a spontaneous applause at such natural beauty?"

I turned my attention toward her. I looked deeply into her blue eyes. Her eyes searched my face as if she were looking for answers. We could both feel the tension slowly build between us. My pulse quickened. I watched as her chest rose and fell with each rapid breath she took. I didn't lessen my gaze as I let the desire build. After a moment, I slowly leaned in toward her, close enough to smell the key lime pie on her lips and feel her breath on my face. I paused to relish in the intensity as it grew. Still looking in her eyes, I leaned back just a few inches to let the attraction catch its breath and gave her my most seducing of smiles.

She let out a soft sigh of relief, sat back, and collected her thoughts.

"You're an interesting man, Alexander," she said, trying

to regulate her breath. She placed her empty dish down on the stone wall and stood up and wiped the crumbs off her white shorts. "This was very nice, but I need to go. I have an early day at work tomorrow." Her words came out a little too fast. She sounded flustered.

She gathered her things into her macramé handbag. The book she was reading fell to the ground. I quickly bent down to pick it up.

"Poetry?" I asked, flipping through the pages.

"Yes," she answered. "When I came down here last night, there was an old local writer, William J." She looked at me and raised her eyebrows. "You probably know him too, right?" she said sarcastically. "Anyway, he was reading some of his poems over there," she explained as she pointed toward the corner of Wall Street and Exchange Street. While she talked, I continued to rifle through the pages. I noticed she had a page earmarked. I read it aloud.

> The grass is becoming greener under my feet.
> It is wanted by you but it cannot be.
> For a storm I would create.
> In the end I could not weep.
> For something worked for will not be lost
> By the thoughtless scuffing of feet.
> —William J.

"Hmmm," I said. "Interesting words."

"What can I say? I'm a sucker for interesting words," she stated, retrieving the book from my hands. "So I bought it." She shrugged.

"So you did," I said.

There was another pause between us. I took advantage of the lingering desire.

"May I walk you home?" I asked, my grin provocative. I

could see by her expression that I had crossed the line, so I quickly changed gears and warned, "You never know when Looting Louie and his friends will show up." I nodded my head in the direction of Louie, who now had Old Man Gus join him in begging for change.

She looked at me as if to counter my advances. "That's quite all right, Dr. Alexander."

"It's Morgan," I corrected her.

"Excuse me?"

"It's Dr. Alex *Morgan*."

She smiled. "That's quite all right, Dr. Alexander Morgan. I'm perfectly capable of getting myself home safely—and *alone*."

"How about this Friday?" I immediately followed. "Will I see you at sunset?" Surely, she couldn't resist my charm.

"I thought your only days off were Wednesdays," she said.

Ah, she paid attention. I smiled. *I'll give her a day to miss me.*

"Yes, but I have this Friday off," I lied.

"We'll have to see about that, now won't we, Dr. Morgan?" she teased.

"See you at sunset," I said softly as I gently kissed her on her cheek. She closed her eyes to embrace the moment. I took a step toward her, invading her comfort zone. I drew my face toward hers and placed my hand on the small of her back. I could feel the energy between us course through my body as I whispered slowly and deliberately in her ear, "Be here—Friday."

Then I turned to leave and didn't look back. I stuck my hands in my pockets and walked with my head held high, smiling to the clouds above. I couldn't recall when I had ever been this happy.

I knew I was hooked, and I was confident she was too. Her eyes told me so.

> I didn't want to kiss you good-bye—
> that was the trouble—
> I wanted to kiss you good night—
> and there's a lot of difference.
> —Ernest Hemingway

12 Kisses in the Keys

That Friday, the local *Key West Citizen* morning paper published that sunset would be 8:21p.m.

I left work at 3:00 p.m. and took myself off on-call status. Being the chief does have its perks. I even left my Motorola pager at home. Oz had left a note on the kitchen table that he'd be gone until Monday. He added in his note that he'd left my mail on the table and had thrown out everything rotten in the fridge—again.

I took a long, hot shower and changed into jeans and a white collared shirt. I stopped in to see Captain Tony and have my tequila and lime. He gave me an "atta-boy" slap on the shoulder as I walked out of his bar. I tossed a quarter toward the mouth of the fish but missed. I was in too good of a mood to let that bother me, and I walked down Duval toward Mallory Square. I bought a long-stemmed red rose from Paulo, the street vendor I knew well. I had patronized his floral services over the years for many unsuspecting ladies. I walked to the pier and looked around. She wasn't there yet. I grabbed a stool at El Meson's and waited.

It was 6:45 p.m. when I saw her. She had on a blue wrap dress, and her hair was pulled back by a leather woven headband, her skin deliciously tanned from the sun. I left a ten-dollar bill on the counter, grabbed the rose, and walked toward her.

She spotted me walking toward her and nervously waved.

My smile widened as I approached her.

I presented her with the long-stemmed rose I had hidden behind my back.

"What if I didn't show?" she said, taking the rose I offered.

"Ah, but you did," I said as I watched her cheeks blush.

"Have you eaten?" I asked.

"Alexander, this is not a date," she said. "We are just here to watch the sunset."

I just smiled and let her lie to herself.

"Then how about a little key lime pie and a margarita while we watch the celebration?" I countered. She smiled.

"You just sit here." I motioned to the stone wall. "I'll be right back."

I grabbed two slices of pie from Caroline's, two drinks from the vendor next door, and walked back to Vivian.

"Thank you," she said, taking the pie from my hand.

"You are very welcome, Vivian," I said, taking any excuse to say her name out loud.

"So what's your story, Dr. Morgan?"

I was quiet for a moment. She had impulsively used one of my lines on me. Vivian had a knack for catching me off guard. I was accustomed to being the one leading the questions, the one in control. Anyone else prying into my personal life would have me quickly abandoning this evening's romance, but talking to her seemed so natural, like there was nothing I wanted to hide.

"Cat got your tongue, Doctor?" she coyly asked.

"Doctor, is it?" I smiled, trying to buy some time on my answer.

"You're stalling, Alexander."

How does she do that?

"There's no story really," I answered. "I'm from New York and moved down here a few years ago."

"Your family's still up there?"

I sipped on my drink, pondering how I would answer that question. I hadn't seen my mother since I was six and placed in foster care, and I never knew who my father was. *How do I explain that I'm the result of a drug-addicted whore who traded her body for another fix?*

"I guess," I answered. "We're not that close," I said truthfully. "Besides, being a superstar of a doctor kept me in medical school and residency pretty much twenty-four-seven for over seven years." *There you go, Alex. Lighten the mood.*

"I moved down here to finish my surgical fellowship and never left," I said, taking another bite of Caroline's key lime delight with extra meringue. "Once you come to Key West, it's hard to leave." I gave her my most irresistible of smiles.

We talked awhile, and I did my best to avoid any more personal stories. I was a professional at letting others open up, but I was an expert at being closed.

We sat there talking, laughing, and watching the sunset. She told me all about her sister, Gail, whom she told all her secrets to. She told me about growing up as an Irish Catholic in a small New York town where everyone knew everyone. She told me about how much she liked to read poetry and how much Gail liked to read the Bible.

I didn't bring up my past, but I did reveal safe-telling stories about my roommate, Oz, and my terrible housekeeping habits. You'd think being a doctor I'd be meticulous; instead, it was Oz who took care of everything. He'd clean out the fridge at least once a week, empty the trash, and check the mail. I told Vivian how well he and I got along, giving each other space. My only pet peeve about Oz was his love for strays. I complained to Vivian how our backyard was becoming a refuge for all lost animals.

She jokingly asked if I was one of them.

I watched the way her lips danced when she talked, how her eyes lit up when she talked about poetry, and how her eyebrow arched every time she tried to be serious.

All I kept thinking was sitting there, next to her, I could forget the world I knew and live like that forever.

The crowd had dispersed, and the night was growing dark when she interrupted my thoughts and said, "Alexander, I really need to go."

"Do you really?" I questioned.

"I'm afraid so. I have an early day tomorrow."

"The night is still young," I tried to convince her. "And we have all this to still enjoy." I looked around the pier; you could still see the moonlight glistening in the water.

She gave me a smile but shook her head and glanced down for a moment.

I lifted her chin with my hand and leaned my face toward her lips. I wasn't going to pause this time, but somehow she could read my mind again and turned her head, presenting me with her left cheek instead. Obediently, I kissed it and gently turned her chin back, facing me, and looked deep into her blue-gray eyes. I slowly leaned in closer. I could smell the tequila on her breath. I tilted my head closer and kissed her gently. Her lips were softer than I had imagined. I closed my eyes and parted her lips with mine. I could taste the trace of lime. For a moment, she let me, and then suddenly she leaned back, slowly ran her fingers over her lips, and closed her eyes for a moment. She let out a faint sigh and stood up.

"Listen, I really need to go," she said, almost apologizing.

"I'm sorry," I lied. "I just couldn't help myself," I countered with truth.

I slowly reached for her hand and placed it in mine. "I'll walk you home, and I won't take no for an answer."

She looked up at me reluctantly; there went her eyebrow again.

"Well then," I said, acknowledging her response. "I'll just *walk* you there," I said assertively. "I promise, cross my heart."

We held hands as I walked her down Whitehead Street past Hemingway's house and made a right onto Truman Avenue toward the naval base. The night air was humid, and the salty breeze naturally curled her long blonde hair.

We talked about her work and how much headway they were making with cleaning up the contaminated water by using updated biological agents that could break down the oil. I didn't really hear a word she said, but I listened to every single syllable. On occasion, I'd ask a question, and she'd expertly answer in detail, her free hand gesturing her words. By the time we got to the base, I could sense she was growing comfortable with me. Vivian waved, and I smiled as we passed the uniformed night guard at the annex gate who looked at me with suspicion.

When we approached the camp, I looked around at the naval barracks. There were two rows of three-story concrete military buildings with a four-story building at the far end, forming a U-shape. They looked desolate and dreary—no grass, no plants, no shrubs, just a single palm tree in the center court. A bit dismayed, I asked, "You live here? With the marines?"

"Well, not really. Not *with* the marines," she answered. "This particular unit is just for us interns." She pointed. "Those two over there are for the marines that live here." She directed my attention to the row of barracks down the road that had ample amounts of flood lamps illuminating the dirt grounds.

"Oh?" I remarked as I saw two marines walk out their barracks on the far end. Were they waiting up for her to return? I wondered. I could feel a tinge of jealousy emerge.

Vivian continued, "The base is pretty much decommissioned. There's only about thirty or so marines left to close things down. The navy's primary installation in the area is the Naval Air Station Key West, on Boca Chica Key."

"Then I'd say you're pretty safe here," I said. "At least from Looting Louie and his friends anyway."

"Yes, I am." She glared at me. "I can take care of myself." Oh that eyebrow of hers was in full alert.

"I'm sure you can, Vivian. Well good night then. Leaving as promised." I grinned. "Vivian, I had a wonderful evening." I gave a gentleman's bow.

"Yes." She smiled. "I did too." She twirled her rose in her hand.

I leaned in and kissed her on the cheek.

"See you at sunset?" I asked.

"I'm quite busy." A gentle protest.

"I'll see you at sunset, Vivian." I turned to leave.

"But don't you work tomorrow?" she questioned.

I took a few more steps before calling out, "See you at sunset." I didn't turn around. I just waved my hand in the air, knowing she was watching.

The whole way home, I couldn't help but have this ridiculous grin plastered on my face. Yup, she was hooked too.

13 Shift Change

I managed to adjust my ER schedule with Clark Abelman, who was all too eager to pick up my hours. We had a great working relationship. I did everything, and he picked up my leftovers. He was a hotshot surgeon from Washington who arrived at Memorial shortly after I became chief. I could tell he had his sights set on my position ever since he had heard the rumor. The hiring committee had hinted at the possibility of my position becoming available in the not too distant future. The rumor was that I'd burn myself out in no time. That my addiction, my passion for my job would—what was that myth about Atlantis? Oh yeah, that I would sink under the weight of my own perfection. That wasn't about to happen. That was a myth. I was a legend. My skills defended my arrogance, and they knew it. But now with my addiction placed elsewhere, it was his opportunity, his chance to shine. I still worked twelve-hour days, but I was out the door by 6:00 p.m. I took off Wednesdays and Sundays, and surprisingly, when I was away from the hospital, I didn't even miss Memorial. Clark was perfectly capable and willing to take care of all her needs.

The next night, and most of the nights that week, I met up with Vivian at the pier. I'd get the drinks, and she'd stop at Caroline's for two slices of key lime pie. We watched the sunset together and let it dazzle and amaze us. Each sunset was its own distinctive dance. No two were alike. We'd talk, we'd laugh, and we'd sit in silence, her head resting on my shoulder. Afterward, like clockwork, I'd walk her home, leaving her with just a kiss on her cheek and a yearning for wanting more.

The following Friday night, I showed up with Oz.

She looked surprised but happy to see us both.

"We are *all* going out to dinner tonight," I stated. "I brought Oz along with me to make sure you would say yes."

"Well, with that, how could I say no?" She chuckled.

We walked to Seven Fish, my favorite restaurant on the corner of Oliva and Elizabeth Street. It was equally distant from home and the hospital. Oz and Vivian hit it off immediately and chatted the whole way. Oz had such a calming presence and had such a deep insight into people. He seemed to really enjoy all the questions Vivian rattled off.

By the time we walked to the restaurant, I was hungry. Kim-Ly sat us at my regular table, and I ordered the wahoo fish with angel pasta flavored in mango and papaya. Honestly, I didn't even know if they served anything else. Oz and Vivian both had the yellowtail snapper.

Our conversation flowed easily among the three of us. She and Oz were deep in a conversation about different animal species that are threatened with extinction due to man-made evils when our server, Kim-Ly, interrupted their heated discussion. She kindly asked if we would mind taking our conversation elsewhere. Apparently, it was well after closing time, and the last table had left over an hour ago. We apologized for taking so much time and left the restaurant. I was so relieved when I heard Vivian promise Oz that she was interested in seeing the collection of stray wildlife he was trying to save in our backyard on Pauline Street.

Oz introduced Vivian to all the creatures in the back while I opened a bottle of wine and sat out on the front porch. The evening couldn't have gone any better, I thought to myself, taking a sip of wine. I looked up at the dark sky and then closed my eyes; for the first time in my life, I felt serenity in my soul.

We continued our evening on our front porch, sipping a bottle of cabernet while their conversation turned more esoteric. Their discussion on animals morphed into what animal signs meant and what their spirit animals symbolized.

I was completely out of my element and just sat as a quiet observer. Oz told us about hummingbirds and that their spirits symbolize the joys of life and lightness of being. I just nodded in agreement, content to be sitting there next to Vivian.

Vivian looked enchanted, her eyes bright with interest. "It's fascinating too that these tiny birds are capable of the most amazing feats, despite their size. And they travel great distances with the ability to easily move from one place to another," she added.

Not to be completely removed from the discussion, I said, "Well you are obviously a butterfly."

"Oh yeah?" Her eyes narrowed.

"Yeah. You're beautiful, graceful, colorful, and you constantly move your wings—I mean, hands—nonstop." I couldn't contain my laugh as I flapped my hands in the air like a bird. She slapped my arm in protest.

Oz just smiled and shook his head. He told us both that a butterfly was symbolic of a soul. Vivian jokingly added that my spirit animal was an owl, old but wise. I just smiled and enjoyed the banter of the conversation and refilled all our glasses. As I was about to get up and retrieve another bottle, Oz mentioned that an owl can give you new eyes in which to see, to show you things that otherwise might remain hidden. Sometimes it was hard to follow what Oz said; he always seemed to say more than the words he used. I went to go see if I could find a hidden bottle of wine in the kitchen.

We all sat on the porch drinking and talking until two in the morning. Vivian eventually fell asleep in my arms as Oz and I discussed once again what to do about all the animals accumulating in our backyard. We finally called it a night around three. I carried Vivian into my room and tucked her in under the sheets. I grabbed a pillow from the bed and slept on the couch.

At 6:00 a.m. I had left her a pot of coffee with a note that read:

> *I wouldn't dare wake you, my little butterfly*
> *spirit. See you at sunset.*
> *–Alex*

14 The Owl and the Butterfly

I know she tried to fight it. I have to give her credit for that. But the attraction was too strong for either of us to resist. Love is a drug no matter how you look at it, and she was now dependent on me, and I was at her mercy. It wasn't long before my pillow and I joined her in my bedroom, and I no longer slept on the couch.

We spent every day together we possibly could. We'd watch the sunset and stroll for hours talking. I opened up a little bit more about my past, and she would just listen. Some days Oz would join us for dinner, or we'd all just sit on the porch and talk the night away. We always seemed to stay at my little cottage on 701 Pauline Street rather than her place at the Naval Station. I just assumed it was because she felt home there.

Sometimes I'd watch her sleep, just looking at her face. She was so stunning. The smell of her skin, her blonde hair carelessly thrown over my chest, her heart beating with mine.

I never said those three words aloud, and either did she, but our hearts had their own code that bound us together. I was confused and uncertain about how I had gotten here. I'd never been this close to anyone. I had never let anyone in. The way we touched, the way we connected, I swear we had become one.

* * * *

"Happy two-month anniversary!" she said one Wednesday morning, bringing in a tray of pancakes, eggs, and bacon in bed. The hospital schedule change with Clark Abelman was working out well; he was thrilled running the show, and I couldn't have been happier. The time I spent with Vivian was addicting.

"Wow, breakfast in bed. I could get used to this," I said, grabbing a piece of bacon off the plate. Next to the coffee was a small box wrapped in yellow ribbon from Avery's trinket store down the road.

"What's this?" I held up the box and yellow envelope and shook it, trying to guess the contents.

"Oh just something I picked up. It's nothing special really, but I just couldn't help myself." She giggled. "I got something for Oz too. I left his in the kitchen."

She bounced into bed next to me. I sat up and opened the box.

Inside the small box was a small porcelain owl with small imperial topaz gemstones as eyes. It stood on a small pewter perch that had "Wisdom" and "Protector" engraved.

I looked at her and frowned, "Old owl am I?"

"No, silly. You're wise and my protector." She giggled and kissed me firmly on the lips.

Her eyes were bright. Her smile illuminating. She was so happy.

"Well in that case, thank you!" I said and pecked at her lips. I looked into her eyes and then took my time kissing her soft lips, the taste of maple syrup on her tongue. I opened my eyes only to get lost in hers.

I know she loves me. Her eyes tell me so.

I reached over and pulled her down on the bed and kissed her again. She glanced up at the clock on the nightstand; it was 8:45 a.m.

"Oh no, not again," she cried. "I'm so late." She jumped out of bed and ran into the bathroom and shut the door. I could hear the shower turn on.

I smiled and sat up to eat my breakfast. I reached over and opened the card. It read:

> Alexander, my wise owl,
> As long as you watch over me, I am protected.
>
> See you at sunset,
> Your little butterfly

A little piece of paper fell out of the card. It was a preprinted description card that came with the owl.

> Avery's Antiques and Treasures
> 518 Fleming St., Key West, FL 33040
>
> Owls are birds from the order Strigiformes. They are large nocturnal birds of prey with sharp talons. They are found in all regions of the earth. Throughout many cultures, the symbolic meanings of owl include intelligence, perspective, quick wit, independence, wisdom, protection, mystery, and power.

I flipped the card over and read:

> Owl: The Spirit Animal
>
> The owl spirit has a strong connection with the element of air. Their vantage point allows

you to open doorways into other realms and connect with ancestors, angels, and the divine.

You cannot deceive the owl, which is why this spirit animal reminds us to remain true to ourselves. Owl does not tolerate illusion or secrets. If there are skeletons in the closet, you can trust that owl will find them. Some regard the owl as a conjuror who is silent and fierce, and who foretells the oncoming of death.

Well I'm not sure I like all that.

I placed the tiny owl and the card on the nightstand. The card fell to the floor next to her books. I got up to retrieve the card and noticed a poem she had been working on. I read her handwriting:

Crystals shattering into perfect fragmented pieces of time
… Destruction …

But still reflecting the beauty of the sunset.
Soon to be turned into sand shifting on the shore.

Sometimes I didn't understand Vivian's taste in poetry or her poems; they always seemed to leave me a bit uneasy. I finished eating the breakfast she had made. I smiled listening to her sing along with the radio blaring Looking Glass's hit song "Brandy."

Ha, I thought to myself as she continued to sing. *She certainly is a fine girl, and what a good wife she would be.*

Then August happened.

15 Addiction: Hitting Bottom

*I*t was Monday, August 22, 1977. I was taking a quick nap in the doctors' lounge. I was on the twentieth hour of my twenty-four-hour shift when my pager went off. The PA came on, always a bad sign. I'd been at the hospital all weekend. In addition to the normal chaos of the weekends in the Keys, there was an art festival, a rock concert, and three cruise ships docked at the pier that weekend. There was no way Clark could handle the influx all by himself. I stayed on for the additional twenty-four-hour shift. I was sound asleep on the couch when my pager went off and the intercom blared, "There has been a fire at the marine barracks located on the Truman Annex of the naval air station. Eight people are injured, twelve have smoke inhalation, and three have third-degree burns. We have numerous inbound. All staff to stations."

The announcement repeated, and I tore down to the ER.

My first thought was Vivian.

I looked at my watch. It was 4:21a.m.

We were told by dispatch that around three in the morning the entire barracks were engulfed in flames, source unknown. Fire trucks and ambulances were on the scene. Everything inside the dorms was destroyed in the fire.

I ran to the emergency room and barked to the ER senior nurse, "Check the list for a Vivian Reynolds."

She blankly looked up at me.

"Now!" I commanded. "Vivian Reynolds."

The nurse quickly scanned the list, "She's here … trauma, surgery."

I ran down the hall scanning the rooms. "Who has Vivian Reynolds?" I hollered, passing each trauma unit.

"OR 3!" I heard Clark shout out.

I ran in the room. Clark was at the scrub sink.

"She has a penetrating trauma, an impaled object in her left thigh. Probably a steel pole, which she landed on after jumping from her second-story window. She's also being treated for smoke inhalation and second-degree burns," he calmly stated. He was already scrubbed and ready to go in. "I've got this, Alex." he assured me.

I had been scrubbing in to assist, but he shook his head. "Alex, I've got this. I'll take care of her. There's a male, twenties, with a blunt force abdominal trauma that is showing signs of hypovolemic shock that needs you in 2." He held up his sterile hands and walked into OR 3.

Clark was a great surgeon, and I knew she'd be in good hands. I'd have to go see her after she was admitted. My focus immediately returned to work, and I was in surgery for the next ten hours.

I kicked into addict mode: greet and treat, move 'em in, move 'em out. We treated the twenty stable patients efficiently, released them, and kept the burns onsite. No fatalities.

* * * *

After post-op check on my patients, I headed to the patient rooms to see Vivian. I was going to convince her to move into my place, where she'd be safe and out of harm's way. I'd give her a stern scolding and lecture her about playing with matches. I smiled as I thought of us talking and making plans about where all her stuff would go. What animals she could name and which ones she and Oz had to release back into the wild.

I was so relieved she was okay. Clark said everything went well, no complications. She could go home tomorrow under my care. Now I could take care of her. I was needed. She needed me.

I walked down the hallway toward her room. I was just outside her door, about to walk in, when I heard voices from inside her room.

"I should have never let you stay down here all by yourself," a male voice said. "I told you I could come down more often. Lily and Becca said you were fine, but I just knew this was too long to be apart." His voice sounded shaken. "Gail said you were working long hours, that it would be a waste of time if I came to visit. But look what happened!" Now his voice sounded frantic.

I stood outside and just listened.

"I can't live without you anymore. This fire scared the crap out of me." He continued, his voice anxious, "I should have done this months ago."

I didn't hear Vivian say anything. Maybe I had the wrong room. It had to be. Then I heard the male voice say, "Vivian Elizabeth Reynolds, will you marry me?"

I heard Vivian's exasperated gasp, "Philip!"

I couldn't take another second. Impulsively, I walked into the room. There he was kneeling down by her hospital bed. A diamond ring lay in a red velvet box in the palm of his right hand. He was younger than I was, with sandy blond hair and bell-bottom jeans.

I just stood, frozen, watching from the doorway. I'm not sure if I was in shock or disbelief, but all I could manage to do was stay quiet and stand still. Vivian looked at me, and Philip quickly turned around and walked swiftly toward me and vigorously shook my hand.

"Doc, thanks so much for saving my girl. I can't thank you enough!" he said, still shaking my hand. "I knew this semester here wasn't a good idea—right, Doc?" His grateful demeanor caught me off guard. I looked down at our hands, still shaking, and then at his face so relieved I was there.

"Well, this little episode showed me how much I can't live without her. I took the first flight out of White Plains to make sure I never let her out of my sight again." He looked back at Vivian lovingly and then turned quickly back to me. His tanned skin enhanced his blue eyes as he spoke. "So when can we bust outta here so I can take her home?"

"Uh …" I stammered.

"Doc, can she go home tomorrow?" he asked.

"Home?" was the only word I could get out as I looked back at Vivian.

"Doc, I've only been down here once since she's been here and long-distance phone calls just don't cut it, ya know? What kind of relationship is that? Right, Doc?" he rambled. "When can we jet? When can I take my girl home?" He was almost begging.

I looked past Philip at Vivian while he spoke.

Tears streamed down her face, but she never said a word. Her head just kept shaking back and forth as if to say, "I'm so sorry."

But even through her tears, her eyes kept telling me what I needed to know. She loved me, and I'd never felt more searing pain than I did right at that very minute.

"Doc!" Philip interrupted. "When can I take my girl home?"

I just looked at them, assessing what was before me. Outwardly I kept my composure, but on the inside, I snapped. I took a breath in, and when I exhaled, Alex the Freak, the addict's son, the coldhearted doctor returned. I placed my hand on Philip's shoulder and gave him just that hint of compassion as I looked directly in his pleading eyes. "I'm afraid it's not my call; I'm not her doctor," I said coldly. "Dr. Abelman is. I'll go get him."

With that, I turned my back and walked out. I never looked back.

*   *   *   *

Addicts never lose a taste for their drug; they only become recovering addicts until they fall off the wagon, or that wagon lands on the rooftop of a hospital on a cold December night.

16 Trash, Crash, and Code Red

*A*fter that scene in August, I quit Vivian cold turkey. Clark told me Philip had left the hospital with Vivian the following day, and that was the last thing I knew. I never returned her calls, and I never opened her letters. I just threw everything that was us in the trash.

I buried my head in work. Again. I worked outrageous hours like I had back in Columbia. I rarely watched the sunset anymore. I didn't hang out at Tony's even on my days off. My ego was shot, my drive was gone, and all I had left was my brains. I turned out to be such a disappointment to Captain Tony; all I had left was my skill. All I had was this hospital. My Memorial.

My faithful wife needed me, and I never needed her more. She healed me. Once again, she was my lifeline. We fit. We danced in seamless harmony. It was the perfect relationship. There was no guilt, no remorse; we just got back into the groove. I was home here at Memorial, and she welcomed me with open arms.

My only friend left was Oz, and I kept my distance from him too. He gave me the space I needed to heal. He'd go about the house quietly picking up after me. He'd wash the dishes and the counters, mop the floors. He'd check the mail, he'd bring me home dinner from the Seven Fish restaurant, and on occasion he'd let me just sit there in silence on the front porch drinking tequila as he smoked his cigars. Oz even left a stack of letters from Vivian on the kitchen table, next to the small owl box from Avery's, wrapped in yellow ribbon. Every unopened letter that I'd throw out, he'd salvage. Every memory I tossed, he'd save. He held on to what I so desperately tried to let go.

But by the early 1980s, I began losing interest in good old Key West Memorial. It was the same old homeless vagrants that piled through my ER doors. Looting Louie and his friends, sunburned tourists, and stomach bugs from the cruise ships started to bore me. I wasn't challenged anymore. Clark was still eager to take my position, and I was ready to move on. Memorial would be in good hands. Clark was a damn good doctor, and he'd shine for sure. I still struggled. I tried desperately to recapture my arrogance. Hemingway said that the world breaks everyone, and afterward, some are strong at the broken places. I wasn't strong there either. I had failed even my egotistical self. The mere thought of walking down to Mallory Square made me tremble. I knew the triggers. I knew the signs. I knew it was time to leave. I'd done everything I could possibly do here.

* * * *

In 1985, I received a job offer to be the hospital chief of a new hospital up in New York. One of my foster families had recently written me from up there that my biological mother had died of a drug overdose. I never went to the funeral; to me, she had died over thirty years ago.

I decided to take the job offer, and I moved back north

where I could be more useful, where it would be more interesting, where sunburned tourists didn't exist. Where I wasn't bored.

I was looking forward to this new state-of-the-art medical facility. I wanted to be challenged. I wanted to be needed. I was told that Westchester General Hospital would be known as *"the* hospital of choice by all standards" to everyone within a hundred miles.

I said good-bye to Oz and packed my bags. I bought a condo a mile from the hospital. I attended the fancy ribbon-cutting ceremony in September when they first opened their shiny, chrome, automated doors.

Westchester General became my new love. She was vibrant, bold, and daring. We'd see cases no one else would touch. We had all the modern medical advancements I could possibly ask for. We had the first pulse oximeter in the United States. Rather than drawing blood, this state-of-the-art medical device provided a noninvasive way to measure a patient's oxygen saturation level through wavelength measurements. We acquired the newly developed automated external defibrillator. It claimed to dramatically increase survival rates—up to 70 percent—by using electricity to stop cardiac arrhythmia and help the heart reestablish a solid rhythm. We were the first hospital to carry only brand-new safety needles and syringes, thereby limiting the number-one cause of blood-borne infections, the needle stick. We certainly were something special, and there was already a long waiting list of doctors wanting to work at General.

My new home. And I at its helm.

I handpicked Gray myself out of the long list of potential doctors. He was young and skilled, a hungry mini-me. He followed me everywhere I went and assisted me in every surgery I performed. Gray and I got along great. He was a quick learner and genuinely cared for his patients. A bit too much if you ask me. I told him, "Just a hint of compassion, Gray; a hint is all you need."

Besides Gray, I stayed distant from everyone. I had no family left, and Oz was still at our old house on Pauline Street. I had nothing and no one to tie me to the past, nothing until that night, December 20, 1985. I still couldn't believe that was her in the ICU.

It was her.
She was alive.
It was Vivian.
She was still as beautiful as I had remembered.

I didn't leave her side all night, just sat in the ICU next to her, waiting for her to come out of her medically induced coma. I watched her as she lay there, my mind and emotions racing. All my feelings came rushing back, like not a moment had passed. All those memories in Key West—the highs, the love, the betrayal.

The addiction.

Jackie, the head nurse, had just left to retrieve Vivian's next dose of antibiotics. No matter what Gray said, I stayed planted in the chair next to her bed. I sat there watching Vivian and monitoring her condition. Her breathing was still irregular. Her vitals were still critical.

When I wasn't looking at the monitors, I studied her face. Time had been kind to her. Her hair still long and blonde, her face still striking. I reached to hold her hand in mine and felt her ring. Her diamond ring. Vivian had married Philip.

Philip. Shit. I must tell her about Philip.

Her eyes fluttered as she began to regain consciousness, her eyes trying to focus and discern where she was. She opened her eyes as she looked around the room. Confused and in pain, she moved her head and saw me sitting there so close to her. Vivian's eyes were as blue as ever. As our eyes connected, I could feel her reach deep, back into my soul. I thought my heart was about to explode. I searched deep in her eyes, the eyes that told me they'd always love me, the eyes that froze time. Those eyes were looking back at me.

I couldn't bear to tell her about Philip right now. Maybe I was being a vulture, but I just wanted this moment for myself. I just wanted a few minutes with her, here in the past.

She looked up at me. A small tear rolled down her cheek. She grimaced as she took a small breath in. She tried to talk but let out a small, crackling cough instead.

"Shh," I softly said as I wiped the tear from her face. "You've been in an accident. You're at Westchester General, in the ICU," I said as I cradled my hand lightly against her cheek.

She painfully cleared her throat and said, "Alexander, is it really you? After all these years." Her voice was labored. She was having a hard time breathing.

"Shh," I repeated. "You really shouldn't talk. Just rest," I told her, tucking her blonde hair behind her ear.

She groaned as she tried to move her head, looking around the room. She looked confused.

"Don't move, Vivian. You and Philip were taken here by helicopter last night." I began to tell her what happened. I had to. I couldn't keep it from her anymore. The past was over; she had moved on. She had married Philip. "You and your husband were flown here last night," I began.

"Philip?" Her voice trailed off.

"Yes. Philip. You were both in a serious car accident, and I took care of your husband while …" I began explaining.

Staring at me, her eyes were expressing regret. "Oh,

Alexander, I wanted to tell you. But I—" Tears rolled down her cheek.

"That was a long time ago," I said gently as I dried her tear-stained face. I didn't want to tell her what happened last night, but she had to know.

She seemed to be lost in time as well. She looked at me and said, "I'm so sorry, Alexander. I didn't know what to do." She started to ramble. "And then you never called me back, you never responded to all the letters I sent you. I never got to say—"

"Shh, Vivian," I interrupted her. I could see the stress was taking its toll on her body. Her heart rate was climbing, and her breath became shallow. "Just rest, Vivian. I'm here. I won't leave."

She faintly smiled. "See you at sunset," she said as she reached for my hand. With that, I was free-falling back with her to Mallory Square like an addict finds a vein. Her heart gave life back to mine. Lost in memory, I smiled back at her.

"See you at sunset," I said, my emotions bursting, I ever so softly kissed her hand repeatedly.

"Alex, I have to tell you—"

"Shh ..."

"No, I have to tell you." Her breath had become increasingly labored. Her pulse was racing. She pulled my hand and drew me close.

I leaned in, close enough to kiss her lips just one more time. "What is it, Vivian?" I tenderly asked.

As her eyes welled up with tears, she faintly whispered in my ear, "I have always loved you, Dr. Morgan. I never stopped." She tried to smile.

I could hear her labored breathing; it was strenuous. Her hand reached for my face, and she looked deeply into my eyes. Tears streamed down her face. With little breath left, she grimaced and forced herself to whisper, "She has your name."

At that moment, all the monitors she was connected to alarmed. Her eyes rolled back into her head. Her body started going into convulsions. She was crashing again.

Shit!

She was coding.

Shit!

"Code red!" I screamed. "Code red!"

I flew into action. I was not going to lose her again. Not now. Not that I had her back. I just told her I would never leave.

She had just told me she loved me.

In seconds, the intensive care unit filled with doctors and nurses. Gray grabbed the paddles, and Jackie injected her with a 50 cc shot of epinephrine through her IV.

"Clear!" Gray shouted. Everyone stepped back for a second as the defibrillator tried to shock Vivian back to life.

No response. She was in cardiac arrest and unconscious.

"Clear!" Gray shouted.

No response.

Gray began to give her mouth-to-mouth while I gave her chest compressions.

Jackie stood there with the kit, ready to do an endotracheal intubation if we could give her the ten seconds she needed between the chest compressions.

"Doc?" she asked, holding the bag marked Intubation.

"No! Not now, Jackie," I snapped.

"Five and six and seven and eight—" I continued with my hands, locked together, pushing down in steady rhythm on her chest.

I don't know how much time lapsed when the activity in the room started to slow or at what point they started to clear out of the ICU. I had not slowed my pace, my rhythm precise.

"And twenty-one and twenty-two and twenty-three," I counted.

"Alex ..." Gray's tone was gentle.

"One and two and three and four and ..." I called out, still firmly pushing against Vivian's chest.

"Alex, we did all we could." Gray's tone was calm.

"Twelve and thirteen and fourteen and ..." I ignored him.

He gently put his hand on my shoulder.

"Get the fuck away!" I screamed and forcefully shrugged his hand off my shoulder, my hands still pushing on her chest. Sweat trickled down my face.

"Damn it!" I screamed. I had lost count.

I attempted to start again. "One and two and three and ..." I trailed off.

I looked around the room. Everyone had left but Gray. I looked at him, his eyes in sadness, consoling mine. My eyes widened in disbelief. I quickly scanned the monitor for confirmation of her vitals. The machine was shut off. I looked down at Vivian. Her body was limp, her face pale.

"No!" I cried. I couldn't take my eyes off her. I just stood there and shook my head in defiance. Not Vivian. "No!" I screamed at her, my head in a furious denial. Not my Vivian, not my soul, not my butterfly.

I had nothing left. All that gave me strength deserted my body. What shell was left standing collapsed on top of her lifeless body. Though I could barely breathe, I held my Vivian and wept uncontrollably.

Vivian Elizabeth Reynolds Crenshaw was pronounced dead at 11:02 a.m. on December 21, 1985.

* * * *

I didn't know it at the time, but when your heart is completely and utterly destroyed, you learn to live in a way you never knew you could live before. The truly wise know that love is the greatest gift, the most painful of scars, and that true love never, ever ends.

17 *Parker and the Storm*

The thunderous sound of a helicopter approaching invaded the room. It was the first of July as Jenna looked out her window of room 313 and saw the MedEvac chopper landing on the roof above the emergency room section of the hospital, its long blades spinning above the belly of the helicopter as it lowered toward the rooftop. Its silhouette was black, like an insect set against the sky and the setting sun.

The helicopter landed. Jenna's eyes were still fixated out the window. She saw Dr. Ava Mendoza, General's chief pediatric surgeon run out to the roof, her arms urgently waving in the technician who was pushing the gurney toward the rooftop elevator. Nurse Ellen pushed a filled syringe into the flimsy IV that they had inserted once inside the MedEvac. Jenna could see the patient was a boy, about her age, and his face and legs looked covered in blood. They wheeled the boy through the double doors on the rooftop, and they were gone.

Jenna turned from the window and looked at her mother, "Looks like we got another taker here at Club Med." She motioned out the window. "This kid got the special super-deluxe escort from Dr. M. No passing Go, no getting $200.

The direct line straight to the OR. What's the over-under that he'll be my next roomie by day's end?"

"Jenna, we really have to work on your vocabulary. People will start thinking you were raised in a casino," Mary cautioned.

"So, that's a 'no' bet?" Jenna mocked.

There was a knock at the door, and Dr. Grazer popped his head in and smiled.

"What do you think about heading home tonight?" he asked Jenna.

"What? Really?" Jenna beamed at Dr. Grazer.

"I'll have Madelint call in your meds to New York Home HealthCare and see if we can't finish this at home," he stated. "What do you say? Home by dessert?"

Jenna sprung up out of bed and immediately started to shove her games and M&Ms into her book bag.

"Well, I guess that answers your question," said Mary, looking at Dr. Grazer.

"Okay, I'll get working on the discharge papers. Ellen will be in to go over all the follow-up details, and Madelint will give you a call to set up delivery with Home HealthCare. They'll need to set up an appointment first thing tomorrow morning with the at-home nurse."

"Thanks, Doc! Love to stay but—nah, I'd be lying," Jenna joked as she finished shoving all her belonging into her duffle bag.

"Okay, Ma, let's roll!" Jenna said to Mary, standing with her bags in tow.

"We may need just a few more minutes before we can leave, Jenna," Mary said, smiling at her daughter.

Jenna was discharged shortly after her dinner tray arrived. It was just enough time to finish her double order of spaghetti and meatballs with extra cheese and her two chocolate pudding cups. She never did meet her new roommate who had come in from the rooftop, but somehow she knew his story. She wished she could have been there to help him in some way. He'd be frightened; first time in, first time scared. She knew that. She knew that he'd need a friend. She also knew she wanted to go home.

*   *   *   *

Parker was wheeled in later that night, his father watching anxiously as the rolling gurney was moved from the recovery room into Parker's hospital room. The room had been meticulously cleaned. Both beds were tucked securely with white sheets and blankets that smelled strongly of bleach. Both beds had one white pillow. Both tray tables had the same tent card: "Cleaned today—General Hospitality #701."

"Sweet," Parker said as they wheeled him to the bed by the window. "I bet that's where I came in," he said, looking at the emergency room's rooftop out his window. He picked up his cell phone and took a picture of a helicopter parked on the helipad rooftop. "I'm so sending this to Eric. He's going to be so jealous I got to ride in that helicopter. #BeatThat #SweetRide."

"Sweet?" Mason's tone was serious. "Let's never do *that* again."

Parker looked at his father, who was exhausted. His clothes were rumpled, and the stress of the day left him in need of a shower; his five o'clock shadow was gray, his eyes bloodshot. Mason Harris let the plastic bag marked "Hospital Belongings" drop to the ground as he slumped into the chair with a heavy sigh. He took his phone out of his pocket.

Six missed calls.

Seventeen texts.

He searched his shirt pocket for his reading glasses. He hated that he had to wear them, but he also couldn't figure out how to increase the font size on his phone. He couldn't decide which was worse—the damn glasses or the ridiculous too-small phone font.

There was a knock at the door. "Mr. Harris?" asked a young nurse.

"Yes?" he answered, taking off his reading glasses.

"Will you be spending the night with your son?"

"Yes." He looked over at Parker laying in the hospital bed. "But I doubt he'll let me squeeze in there with him."

"Ah, no, Mr. Harris," she answered sweetly. "I'll go grab some sheets and towels from the bin right here outside your door. I'll grab some towels in case you want to shower; it's right down the hall. I'll be back in a moment to show you how to convert that chair you're sitting in into a bed."

"This?" he said inquisitively as he looked at the chair he was sitting in.

"Yes, absolutely," she said in a cheery voice.

"Okay then. Thank you. I appreciate it." He smiled and gave a wave as she shut the door.

"You still got it, Dad," Parker joked. Parker's leg was in a cast, and his face had two slashes across his left eye that had been stitched. His neck was in a brace, but he still was able to move around with ease.

Mason looked at his son and chuckled. "Got it, do I? *Ha,*" he said, shaking his head as he put his reading glasses back on and squinted as he attempted to read his texts. He was soon distracted by the commotion coming from the hallway right outside Parker's room.

"I am looking for room 313," said a woman's voice loudly.

"My son is in there. Is there anyone here able to show me where his room is?" she demanded.

"Ma'am, do you have a visitor's pass?" said an elderly woman.

"*Ma'am?*" she mimicked back. "Yes, as a matter of fact, I do; it's called being his *mother*. And yes, I went through Fort Knox over there by the elevator by a very disgruntled security personnel. You may need to review your hiring policies," she said even louder.

"Ma'am, I *do* need to see your pass," said the same elderly woman's voice.

"For crying out loud, here's the damn pass," she growled. "Now, where is Parker Harris?"

"Oh crap," Parker said to his father. "Mom's here."

* * * *

Some storms roll in like hurricanes, and it's best to just brace yourself and await impact.

18 The Storm Arrives

*T*he hospital door flung open, and Parker's mother strode in. She was an attractive fifty-year-old woman dressed in a crisp, size-too-small white blouse, blue pencil skirt, and three-inch navy blue heels. Her brown hair was pulled back and secured in a twist, her black-rimmed glasses were positioned like a headband in her hair, and a red scarf was tied around her neck. Her blue blazer had a pin on its lapel, and it hung neatly over her forearm. Her designer leather pocketbook slung over her shoulder as she clutched a pink paper hospital pass in her left hand and her cellphone in her right.

She looked directly at Parker and let out a long exhale of relief.

"Hi, Mom," Parker said casually.

"Hello, Helen," Mason said coldly.

She walked past Mason, threw her stuff on the edge of the Parker's bed, and put her manicured hands on her hips. "Parker, what the hell were you thinking! You scared me half to death." Her voice sounded angrier than usual. "I didn't get your text until I landed in LAX. Did you intentionally wait until I was halfway across the country to do this to me? I had to wait for two standby flights before I could get the DTW connection to Westchester." She glared at Parker and took a quick breath.

"And then I had to switch my LAX shift with Luanne, and I will probably owe her my next child for that favor. I should just tell her to take you, since you don't listen to a damn thing I say anyway."

Parker knew better than to interrupt his mother when she was in one of her moods. He stayed silent, lying in his hospital bed, lines and leads connected to him, the monitors quietly beeping.

"And a *text*, Parker?" she sneered an octave higher, and her voice cracked. "What the hell? That's how you tell your mother you've been in an accident and are being medically evacuated to a hospital?"

Parker took a breath and looked at his father and said sarcastically, "Well, that text was from Dad, since I was in the ambulance, and then the helicopter—so ..." His sentence faded.

"Parker Anthony Harris!" she shrieked.

Uh-oh, I may have crossed the line, Parker thought.

Helen looked over at Mason. "For Christ's sake, Mason. I told you I didn't allow him to drive those dangerous contraptions! See?" She pointed to Parker's bandaged leg.

"Helen, it's a four-wheeler, and he's not a baby. He's thirteen. You could be a bit more concerned for your son. He did have quite a day."

"Really?" she scowled. "I can see with my own eyes that he's okay, Mason." She turned again to Parker. "Plus, I talked with doctor what's-her-name while waiting for the Detroit connection."

"See, Mom," Parker tried to bring some levity into the room, "aren't you glad you were in Los Angeles when you got the text? You didn't have to worry as long." He smiled.

"Seriously, Parker, I'm going to kill you." She paused for a minute, scanning Parker sitting in the hospital bed. She let out a heavy sigh and then reached down and hugged him tightly.

"Mom … um, that kind of hurts."

She let go immediately and stood up, straightening her skirt. "Oh, I'm sorry, honey." She sounded almost apologetic.

"Helen, he's fine," Mason assured her.

Helen took a long breath and seemed to regain her composure. She unwrapped her scarf from her neck and carefully folded it. She took a few more deep breaths as she looked down at her son. Her face changed from its usual stern and extremely businesslike expression to one that was more motherly, more emotional. Parker hadn't seen that very often from his mother.

"Thank God, Parker," she said. "I don't know what I'd ever do without you." She put the scarf carefully into her bag. She didn't say a word for a few minutes. No one did. Helen stood at the end of his bed, clearly trying to control her emotions. Parker typed away at his phone while Mason put his glasses back on and grabbed his cell phone.

Helen looked over at Mason. "Now, why the hell did you let this happen?" she said, her tone, accusing. "I told you I didn't want him riding those death traps. We live in Queens, Mason. There's no reason for him to be riding any sort of machine through your Godforsaken country backwoods."

Mason didn't answer. He just looked at her for a moment, then returned his attention back to his phone.

She let out a huff and then walked over to the mirror in the room and looked at her reflection for a moment. Parker saw that her face was tired. He hadn't really noticed when it was exactly that her once-smooth skin had been replaced with lines of worry.

She let out another heavy sigh as she walked back to the bed to retrieve her purse. She grabbed her hairbrush and her makeup bag and tried to conceal what she could. Her brown hair fell as she took out the pins from her hair. She brushed it and twisted it back up and pinned it back into place.

She gave herself a nod of approval.

"Ha," Mason smirked.

"Ha? What, Mason?" she questioned.

"Nothing."

"No really, what?" she pressed.

"You're just ridiculous, that's all. You come in here, guns blazing. You give Parker the riot act after everything the poor kid's been through today, and you are more concerned about the way you look in a hospital than your own son. You're ridiculous. It's always about you."

"Go to hell, Mason."

"And spend eternity with you? No thank you," he quipped.

Helen gave Mason a cold stare.

"Well it'd be a hell of a lot better than living in that damn backward hillbilly town you live in," she sniped.

"You lived there too, or did you forget?" he snapped back.

She looked over at Parker, who was wearing earbuds, pretending to be engrossed in his phone. His music was on, but he could discern the undercurrents in their long-time animosity. No real need to hear every word.

"I'll have you know *I do know* what he's been through," she said, pointing her hairbrush in Parker's direction. "He fractured his femur, he has two lacerations to the face that needed ten stitches each, and his collarbone is broken. They want him to wear that brace for a few days as protective measure. The doctor—what's her name—said Parker needs to stay here until they are confident that there are no residual issues from his concussion. Apparently when he was thrown from the ATV, he was knocked out for over three minutes."

She gave herself another quick look in the mirror and said, "And the doctors tell me he'll recover just fine."

She turned back toward her ex-husband. "Mason, I'm on it. Just because I was working doesn't mean I'm not a good mother." She put her glasses back on.

"I didn't say that, Helen."

"What are you saying then?" she pressed him. "You could have called me. Or at the very least text me what was going on."

"For crying out loud, enough," he said with some heat. "Talking to you is like talking to a crazy person, you know that? You are crazy."

"I'm crazy? You're the one who let him drive that damn thing. You're the one who was supposed to make sure he wouldn't get hurt. You say that I'm crazy?" Her eyes shot him an angry glare. "Yeah, well, maybe you're right, Mason. Maybe I've been crazy my entire life. But so are you, you know that? Perhaps to a lesser degree, but surprise, we're all crazy." She looked over at Parker, then back at Mason and lowered her voice to an angry whisper. "I was crazy enough to marry you, wasn't I? I've been through hell, Mason. You know that. There are days I feel I can conquer the world, and then there are days I can't get my head off the fucking pillow. I live crazy."

She paused, gave herself a last look in the mirror. "Now tell me something I don't already know." She shoved the hairbrush in her bag.

His father just sat quietly and shook his head.

"Well, I don't need to stay here and take this crap," she said in a huff. "I'm going to go to the cafeteria." She reached for her purse. "Parker, do you want anything?" She paused, waiting for an answer from her son. "Parker?" She repeated trying to get his attention.

Parker, still pretending to be engrossed in his cell phone, took out his earbuds and answered, "Nah, I'm good." He put his earbuds back in and began playing the air drums.

Helen grabbed her handbag and opened the hospital room door. She took one step out the door when all the fire alarms on the third floor went off. Startled, she stepped back into the room and peered down the hallway.

Parker sat up in bed and yanked out his earbuds. *What kind of emergency is going on?* Bright strobe lights flashed throughout the pediatric floor, and the sound of the alarm was deafening.

Parker's young nurse ran toward the room, motioning Helen back into the room. "Please remain here, as the floor is on lockdown during the fire alarm. A fire alarm must have triggered the hospital's security system and automatically locked all the fire doors. We'll get this figured out. Don't worry."

Mason stood. "What should we do here?"

"It shouldn't be long," the young nurse yelled over the alarm. "Please shut the door and stay in your room. No one is to go in or out until we find out what happened."

Helen shut the door and leaned heavy against it. She started taking quick and shallow breaths as sweat started to bead on her forehead. She reached in her purse and grabbed a bottle of pills. She opened the prescription bottle and swallowed a tiny white pill without water.

"You okay, Helen?" Mason sounded concerned.

She looked at Mason. "I could really use some fresh air right about now."

"Mom? You okay?" Parker put down his phone. "You don't look so good."

"Honey, I'm fine. It's just been one of those days." She forced a laugh.

"Yeah, I know what you mean," Parker said.

The alarms continued to scream. Mason got up and offered his chair to Helen. She sat down and stared out the window, looking at the emergency room sign that was brightly lit up against the dark night. She tried to wave some air toward her face. Parker saw her take a few deep breaths. Mason poured a cup of ice water from the plastic hospital pitcher and handed it to Helen.

"Here," he offered.

"Thank you," Helen said, taking the cup from his hands.

She took a sip and continued to look out the window, looking up at sky, seeming to concentrate on each breath. Parker felt a little bad; he knew his mom had panic attacks sometimes, and there was very little he could do until the medicine kicked in.

* * * *

Ten minutes went by before there was silence. The alarms had stopped; her emotions calmed. Parker had gone back to surfing music on his phone, and Mason stood underneath the light by the sink, trying to reply to the texts on his phone.

The young nurse popped her head in and said, "Sorry about all that, folks. There was a malfunction in our alarm system. It's probably the new computer system that they put in last week. Computer malfunction." She shrugged. "Anyway, you're welcome to leave the room if you'd like," she said, looking at Helen.

Helen got up to leave again. This time she was calmer and slightly embarrassed. She put on her blazer and straightened her skirt. As she grabbed her leather bag from the counter, two pennies fell to the floor. She picked them up. Both pennies dated 1987.

The year her world fell apart.

She took a deep breath and said, "I'll be back," as she placed her hand on the door. "Right now I could really use some chocolate." She forced a smile. "I'm guessing they don't sell wine downstairs, do they?" She let out a nervous laugh and left the room.

* * * *

I might not know a lot about family dynamics, but I do know it's not about having the time with family; it's about making the time for each other that's important. I didn't mean to alarm you. That's just my two cents.

19 The Connection Flight

*H*elen sat in the corner of the cafeteria with her Diet Coke and bag of peanut M&Ms she purchased from the vending machine. She mindlessly flipped through a style magazine a few times before she decided to go back upstairs. She walked toward the door and tossed the magazine and diet soda into the trash. Her handbag bumped into the corner of the door, and her peanut M&Ms went flying around her.

"Damn it." She bent and began to pick up the loose M&Ms that had scattered at her feet.

"Oh, let me help you. These little guys are valuable." A handsome man in his mid to late fifties came over to help. He bent down next to Helen, holding a cup of coffee.

"Excuse me?" Helen asked as she watched him pick up the peanut M&Ms with his free hand.

"A patient of mine uses these instead of money when she plays Rummy," he said.

"Ah, got it," Helen said. "Better to play with them than to eat them, right?"

"Well, not exactly," he said.

"Thank you, Doctor ..." She paused as she tried to read his embroidered white lab coat. "Dr. Grazer, is it?"

"You're welcome," he said, handing her a handful of peanut M&Ms.

"It's Helen," she introduced herself.

He paused and stared at the pin on her lapel, a pin Helen put on nearly every day for almost thirty years. It was a gold flight pin with a blue globe logo of an airline and the red initials TCA written inside.

"Excuse me?" Helen said, skeptical of what he was staring at.

"Oh, I'm sorry. It's your pin," he muttered. "Is that a pin from TransComAir?"

Helen looked down at the pin and back at Dr. Grazer, dumbfounded.

"Yes. But how would you know that? That airline went out of business over twenty-five years ago. Only employees got these pins. Did you work for TCA when you were younger?" she curiously inquired.

"No." He paused in thought. "No. I was a passenger. I was on one of their planes." His voice grew quiet, as if he were anxious. "I was on the 707 that went down in Phoenix." His eyebrows raised, as if he'd surprised himself by saying those words out loud.

"What? There's no way." Helen gave him a cynical look.

His eyes softened as he pursed his lips and slowly nodded in affirmation.

"Flight 424 out of Phoenix?" Dr. Grazer said.

She nodded.

Helen grew pale as if a ghost of her past stood next to her. "I was on that flight," she said. She reached in her bag, searching. She sighed with relief upon feeling the prescription bottle still there. She took a deep breath, followed by a long exhale. She studied his face. His fair skin looked flushed, and he didn't look familiar to her at all. Surely she would have known him. She searched her mind for some recollection.

He continued, "It was Friday, March 13, 1987. Freddie

Krueger and Jason Voorhees had nothing on that day." He gave a defiant shrug. "I've never flown since."

The silence connected them for the moment. Both were recalling a memory.

After a minute, Helen held up her left wrist and showed him a faded tattoo that read: "Never Be Afraid to Fly" with the TCA logo below it.

He looked at her tattoo, then at her, his eyes wide.

As if in shock, they both instinctively sat at the closest table. He put his coffee down next to her purse.

"I'm a flight attendant. Well, we were called stewardesses back then. For TCA."

He shook his head, staring at her tattoo. He reached for his coffee and took a sip.

"But?" She looked at him, trying to comprehend the conversation they were having. "I would think I'd know you." She was still unsure of his story.

"After the flight ..." Dr. Grazer just shook his head again, as if to gather his thoughts. "After the crash, honestly, I just didn't look back."

"What?" Helen was still confused. "But the group counseling, the survivors' event, the memorial in '94? You didn't go?"

Grazer shook his head again. "No. We'd just left a medical conference in Phoenix and were on the first flight back home to New York."

"What do you remember? About that day?" she asked softly.

He looked at her for a minute before answering. "I've suppressed this for so many years. I'm not sure where to begin."

Helen touched his arm. The white coat he wore was worn of age. Gently, she nodded to encourage his memory.

"There was an explosion about fifteen minutes after takeoff. One of the engines had caught on fire. The pilot—Captain Brenner I think his name was—tried to land right off the Red Mountain Freeway in Rio Salado Park. It was a fifty-fifty toss between landing in the park or the Salt River." He closed his eyes as if every detail was coming into focus.

"I thought we made it when we touched ground, but we … we bounced. And we just kept bouncing." His eyes closed as he spoke. "The nose caught fire, then the tail cracked. The plane just kept bouncing. Then we finally stayed on the ground and slid to a stop." He hung his head and let out a heavy sigh.

She gave him time with his memory. She had learned that in group counseling. Helen knew those details, the bouncing, the fire, but let him talk it through. He clearly needed to share his story.

"There were 158 people on board," he stated. "Twenty-six died, and forty-one were injured." He hung his head. "Me? I walked away without a scratch." He paused. His face softened, his eyes darted up at the ceiling, and he let out a heavy sigh. "My best friend lost his life."

"I'm so sorry." Helen reached across the table to comfort him. She had been in therapy since the crash and had gone over the event a thousand times herself. There was a slight sense of pride within her that she could finally be of comfort to someone else.

She knew sharing her story would help heal the survivors. Her therapist had told her that.

"That was my first year as a stewardess." She offered her story while he sipped on his coffee. "I was young, twenty-two, recently married. I had just finished my six-month probation period, and I finally had more say in my flights. I finally got to decide where to travel, and boy, I wanted to see the world. I had always wanted to see the Grand Canyon, so I took the New York to Phoenix route for the month of March. Three on, three off. Not a bad schedule, and the canyon is beautiful. Even my husband loved it out there." She smiled slightly as she reminisced. Dr. Grazer listened intently.

"Have you ever been to the canyon, Doctor?" She tried to lighten the conversation.

Dr. Grazer shook his head. "No."

They exchanged a glance. Helen added, "Well, you should if you get the chance. It's breathtaking."

"Duly noted." He smiled.

Helen looked back at her wrist, inspecting the tattoo. She didn't look up as she continued, "On that 707 flight, I was on standby hoping to catch that flight back home to New York. The only available seat was in the exit row, so I took it. That's where I was when we hit ground." Her tone became more serious. "On the second bounce, the tail cracked and caught fire. I remember looking at the grass." She paused in thought. "I remember thinking how odd it was to see grass from inside the plane. The suction force was so strong, and we just bounced. The people who unbuckled their seat belts to escape were sucked right into the flames. I just stayed there, frozen. I don't remember how I was knocked unconscious, but the next thing I knew, I was in an ambulance." She shook her head. "In the hospital, they told me I had fractured a few ribs, broken my tailbone, and that I had lost the baby."

Her eyes got teary. "I didn't even know I was pregnant." She grabbed a tissue from her bag, took her glasses off, and carefully dotted the corners of her eyes as to not smear her mascara.

"The docs told me I was lucky to survive. The cockpit and the first five rows were engulfed in flames as soon as we hit. The entire crew and mostly everyone past row 25 didn't survive." She sniffed. "It took over three years for me to get on a plane again, and I'm still in therapy. But I did survive." She choked back. "Of course, my marriage didn't survive, but that's a whole other story." She snickered.

"Right now I'm not sure I love to fly or I just like to run away. I work a lot. Too much if you ask my ex," She confessed. "All I know is that I can't give it up. I've seen hell, and I won't give into fear."

They were quiet for a moment.

"Alex unbuckled," Dr. Grazer said quietly.

"I'm sorry, what?" Helen asked.

"My friend, his name was Alex," Dr. Grazer continued. "We were in seats 24 D and E. Alex saw that a young girl in 23 C had tried to unbuckle her seat belt. He told her not to, but she panicked. She managed to unbuckle her seat belt, but it got tangled, and the young girl was knocked unconscious. Alex went to go buckle her back in. He almost made it, too." He paused, and his eyes welled up. "Until we bounced that one last time."

Helen reached out across the table and held his hands. "Jesus Christ, I'm so sorry."

"Me too." He said holding her hand across the table. "I'm sorry you lost your child."

"Thank you. I lost a baby I never knew I had, and I lost a marriage I couldn't keep. Of course, we were babies ourselves when we got married. Right out of high school. High school sweethearts. Stupid love, really."

She continued with her story.

"Then after the crash, I couldn't deal with anything really. I couldn't deal with people. Mason tried to help. So many people tried to help, but really, I learned that people would rather live in their own contrived reality than deal with yours. My life began to spiral out of control, and the reality is, Doc, people don't want the truth. They want their perception of the truth. Or the truth their own stomachs can handle. They don't want to hear your woes in detail; they just want #InstaLife filtered-down edition of it so they can turn around and tell you in their rehearsed sincerity how much they're praying for you as they head out the door to happy hour and you face death directly in the eyes." Her voice still spewed anger. She opened her hands to the see M&Ms clutched tightly and partly melted. Chocolate smeared her palms and fingers.

She held up her hands. "You can see why I'm in therapy, right?" she tried to joke. She grabbed more tissues from her purse and began to wipe the chocolate off her hands.

"At least you went. I'm not a therapy kind of guy. I never looked back. Once I see fear, I remove it. It's of no use to me. I removed that flight from my mind until now," Grazer confessed.

"Yeah, I shouldn't have looked back either. And I didn't, really. After the divorce, I just traveled the world. Went where I wanted, when I wanted, and with whom I wanted. Then, one morning I woke up and realized I was thirty-six and all alone. I had no one. No family. No one to go home to."

"Funny how that happens," he said.

"Then during one of my annual appointments, my doc reminded me that my biological clock was ticking. That sure did a number on me. I did the only thing I knew to do. I went back home. I went back to my small Hicktown upstate country backwoods looking for my youth. Of course, the only place lonely and desperate single ladies in their late thirties go to feel young again is a bar. The local dive bar on Main Street, USA, where coincidentally ..." Helen used air quotes to accentuate her point, "where *coincidently* I ran into my ex-husband. I spent that summer in an early midlife crisis trying to reclaim my youth with my ex and found out I was pregnant by Thanksgiving." She smiled. "Some luck, huh, Doc?"

"Sometimes someone familiar is what we cling to when we're scared."

"Yes, I think you're right. I was clinging—that's for sure. Anyway, that relationship lasted barely a year. He's still in that same small hometown, and Parker and I moved to Queens to be closer to the hub. I am just meant to fly."

Grazer nodded in agreement. "I'm meant to look forward, not get emotionally attached. Can't let what I can't fix keep me from fixing what I can," Dr. Grazer said. "My old mentor taught me that. 'Move forward,' he'd tell me. 'Love what you do. And never have more than just a hint of compassion.'"

Dr. Grazer leaned in and whispered as if sharing a secret. "Between you and me, I think I'm a much more of a compassionate guy than he'd probably approve of, and I'm definitely a better doctor, too." He smiled.

As he whispered to Helen, a man walking by accidentally bumped into their table and knocked over Dr. Grazer's cup of coffee. The hot coffee poured toward him. Without missing a beat, she added, "And I hope you have a really good sense of humor too." As she tried to wipe up the coffee with her tissues.

$$* \quad * \quad * \quad *$$

Watch what you say. Someone is always listening. And coincidences aren't always a coincidence.

20 Back on Schedule

*H*elen made her way back to the room. The young nurse had somehow converted the chair into a makeshift bed. Both Helen and Mason stayed in the hospital room with Parker—Helen in the makeshift bed, Mason in the wooden chair. The nurse had drawn the center blue privacy curtain to divide the room in two. At some point in the middle of the night, Helen awoke.

She heard muffled voices on the other side of the curtain and listened to the quiet sounds of the whispers as their new roommate was being admitted. Helen recognized a familiar voice; it was Dr. Grazer.

"Your son had a serious asthma attack, so we've admitted him. I know it's his first time here, and we'll take good care of you."

The young woman sobbed, talking through her tears. "Me and my son are all alone. He's got no father. I work two jobs, no time off. Tell me, how do I pay for all this here with him?" She wept softly.

Helen heard Grazer's gentle tone as he comforted the young worried mother and answered every question she had. "I'll give Anu in the billing office a call first thing in the morning and let her know to expect you." Before he left, Dr. Grazer had given his phone number to the mother, telling her to please call him anytime, night or day. Helen smiled at the genuine kindness of Grazer.

Helen looked over at her Parker, sleeping peacefully. She comforted her own insecurities, reminding herself that she was a good mother to her son and she could pay the bills. Lying there, she began to question her life. Had all the years of flying and running away run its course?

She looked at Mason still sound asleep in the wooden chair. She stared at his handsome, rugged face and smiled as she spotted his reading glasses resting on his chest. She recalled the carefree life they had as kids, the laidback routine they lived a lifetime ago. It seemed so easy back then. When did life get so hard and complicated? She watched Mason until she couldn't keep her eyes open anymore.

At 7:00 a.m., Helen awoke to hear Mason talking on the phone with work. His voice was loud. "Yeah, Bill, then they took him by helicopter."

She looked over to see a new nurse listening to Parker's lungs. "All clear," she said cheerfully, wrapping her stethoscope back around her neck. "You had quite the accident, didn't you?" she asked Parker.

Helen shook the sleep from her head and stood up. She straightened the sheets of the makeshift bed and fought the overwhelming feeling that her life had become so foreign to her now.

"I'm going downstairs to get some coffee. Anyone want anything while I'm there?" she asked.

Mason, still on the phone, nodded, gesturing sipping from a cup in his hand. He continued his phone conversation. "I know, crazy, right?" Mason laughed. He still had such a carefree laugh. *How does he do that?* she wondered with a trace of jealously.

"I'm good, Mom," Parker said as he dug into his breakfast tray of sugar cereal and French toast.

Helen grabbed her bag and stopped in front of the mirror. She applied a little foundation under her eyes and took out her hairbrush and began to primp.

Oswin entered as the nurse left to retrieve Parker's chart. He pushed in his mop and bucket and began to clean the room for the day.

Helen brushed her hair and pinned it back up in a twist. She looked long at the reflection in the mirror and decided it was too late to change the path she was on. She dabbed a touch of lipstick on her lips and blotted them. She pushed her face taut, seeing what her face looked like without the wear of life showing, the creases and lines. She let out a sigh and let her face fall naturally as it was.

Oswin mumbled under his breath as he pushed the mop around the room, "The peacock does not like his weakness exposed." And he began to whistle a tune.

She barely heard him and assumed he was just talking to himself. She put her makeup back in her bag and glanced down at the tattoo on her wrist *Never Be Afraid to Fly*. It always gave her strength to read those words. She grabbed her wallet and walked toward the elevator.

When she returned, Dr. Grazer stood in the doorway talking to his young asthma patient. The curtain had been pushed back.

"Well, good morning, Dr. Grazer." Helen balanced the two hot coffees in her hand. She leaned in toward Grazer and said, "And just so you know," she gave him a quick wink, "you do have way more than just a hint of compassion, Doc. That's a good thing, in case nobody ever told you that." She strode over to her ex-husband and handed him a coffee.

"I've got an 11:40 red-eye back to LAX tonight," Helen

said to Parker. "Dr. Mendoza said you'll be discharged later this afternoon. She's happy with your MRI and doesn't think you need to stay here any longer. Isn't that great?" she asked happily.

"Yeah, okay," Parker said a bit listlessly.

"Do you want to stay at Dad's for another week or do you want me to get you tomorrow night when I land?" she asked.

"I'll stay with Dad," Parker decided.

Oswin wiped down the counters and threw away Parker's hospital tray of dinner from the night before—the remnants of a plate of spaghetti and meatballs and two empty chocolate pudding cups. At the base of the garbage, next to the foot petal, he saw what was left of a spray-painted blue carnation. He filled a paper cup with cold water and placed the flower in the cup and whispered to himself, "Love, it go where love is. Love, it have no walls."

He adjusted the flower in the cup, placed it on the windowsill, and left the room. He placed the yellow caution sign near the door, then pushed the mop bucket out into the hallway.

*   *   *   *

It is so common that broken people try to cover up their cracks with anything they can. If only everyone could see the lesson in a flower. It doesn't try to flaunt its beautiful life; it just is.

21 The Collapse

*I*t was the end of August, and Mary and Jenna were back at Westchester. Mary had driven Jenna in just after ten in the morning because she'd awoken early saying her chest really hurt and she was having a hard time breathing. Dr. Grazer met them there in the ER, took one look at her, and said he wanted to run some tests immediately.

Mary and Jenna stayed in the ER bay, Jenna looking so pale, her lips tinged blue. Even at four liters of oxygen, Mary could tell she wasn't getting enough into her system. Jenna complained of a headache and rested her head on Mary's shoulder. Mary heard the crackling in each short breath Jenna took. She had a light haze of sweat on her face; she was clearly working hard to breathe.

Grazer came back in, moving swiftly. He looked over Jenna, using his stethoscope with gentle hands, then turned to Mary. "I need to take her back immediately. I'm afraid it's not good news. The x-rays showed pneumothorax, that her lungs collapsed. We need to try to inflate them, which means we need to get her into surgery. Right now."

Jenna didn't even move; she just left her head resting on Mary as Mary froze in the urgency of his gaze.

"Of course, of course." She nodded, feeling caught in a riptide, a current trying to drag her under. She sat with her daughter in the prep room for as long as they'd allowed her to stay, her hands caressing Jenna's sweet face, watching her small chest rapidly rise and fall with such effort.

Within minutes, Dr. Grazer walked back in with the surgical nurse, their faces serious.

"I'll bring her down to the OR," Grazer said to Mary. "Ava is already scrubbing in, and I'll assist in the surgery. Bridget here is our best surgical nurse, and she'll be out later to update you as soon as possible."

Grazer unlocked the gurney as he began to wheel Jenna out the door. Jenna opened her eyes, looking tired. "I'll see you later, Mama," she said, her voice quiet and hoarse.

"See ya later, baby. I love you, Jenna," Mary said and gave her daughter's small hand a squeeze as she kissed her all over her salty face. Jenna gave her two thumbs-up as she managed a smile. Then the gurney was wheeled away, down the hall and through the double doors. Mary watched until they were out of sight.

She just stood there, tears rolling down her face, lost in all the fear of her mind. She didn't know how long she stayed there when a woman in green scrubs, a nurse she recognized but couldn't place, helped escort Mary to the waiting room.

"Oh, Mary." Her younger sister, Mallory, jumped to her feet as Mary entered the waiting room. "How is Jenna?" she asked, her eyes full of worry.

"Not good, Mal," Mary said with tears in her eyes. "Her lungs have collapsed, and they are trying to inflate them somehow. She's in there with Dr. Mendoza and Dr. Grazer right now. I have no idea how long it will be."

"Oh, Mary," Mallory tried to comfort her sister. "I'm sure Dr. Grazer is doing everything he possibly can to fix it." Mallory looked around the waiting room and asked, "Where's Jim?"

"Out for a run," she said in anger and sat down in the chair. "He said he needed to clear his head before he came here. You know how he is about this place."

"Yeah, I do know. How is it that he can handle a homicide downtown, but this place is too hard for him to deal with? I always told you that *you* were the stronger one." Mallory shook her head. "Well, I'm sure he'll be here as soon as he can."

Mary nodded, not really seeing, not really hearing anything.

"Oh," Mallory said, reaching into her handbag. "Aunt Gail wanted me to bring you this." She handed Mary a worn black Bible.

Mary loved to read everything she could get her hands on—romance, history, autobiographies. She'd read anything, everything, and anywhere. As a child, Mary would read one book after another. She read as an escape after her parents died in a car crash. Even at eight years old, she could never comprehend why Aunt Gail would always tell her, "All the answers you need in life are found in the Good Book." Mary committed herself to read every good book she could get her hands on to find the answer as to why her parents had to leave. Every night, for years, Mary would read sitting in her bed, hiding under covers with a flashlight, searching through the pages. Searching for answers. Searching for God.

Being raised by Aunt Gail was difficult. Mary and her little sister, Mallory, who was barely a year old, went to live with Aunt Gail after the fatal accident. Aunt Gail was caring but stern. She had never married and didn't have children of her own. Mary believed that Aunt Gail tried her best to raise them. On the weekends, Aunt Gail would bake cookies, play board games, and let them have friends over. Mary didn't even mind that she made them make their beds every morning and change out of their school uniforms before they could go outside and play. What bothered Mary the most was that Aunt Gail would never mention Mary's mother by name. Mary and her sister, Mallory, were never allowed to talk about them either. Aunt Gail had set up weekly appointments with Louise Henderson, a grief counselor for Mary. Aunt Gail knew she had to talk to someone about what had happened, but by God's grace, she was not going to be that person. Aunt Gail's reasoning, she'd say, was blessed by God: "Leave the dead to bury their own dead. Go and proclaim the kingdom of God."

What God could there be? Mary would question at night. What God would do this to her? What God could possibly steal her parents from her before Christmas? She was sure there was no Santa Claus, and she was certain there was no God.

Aunt Gail would say, "Now, Mary, remember Luke 10:38." She'd quote yet another verse from the Bible. "You need to be more like that Mary from the Bible and sit at Jesus's feet. Don't be like her sister Martha who ran around being too worried about things. She chose wrong, dear. Don't you." Mary never did read the Bible. She didn't like that Mary in the Bible. When she was asked to pick a name for eighth grade confirmation, she chose the name Martha.

Mary held the worn black Bible in her hands. "Ha. Thanks." She placed the Bible on the novel she had been reading. "I never did read it. Maybe now would be a good time."

"Jenna will be fine," Mallory reassured her sister. She gave Mary a long, comforting hug.

"I'm so glad you're here," Mary said.

"Mrs. Rutherford?" said a female voice from behind the desk.

"Yes?" Mary jumped to her feet walked toward her.

"They just called in from the OR. Dr. Mendoza is still in there with Dr. Grazer. They said Bridget will come out shortly to give you an update."

"Is there anything else?" Mary asked

"I'm sorry, Mrs. Rutherford. That's all they said."

"Thank you, Elise," Mary said. She walked back toward her sister when the emergency room doors opened. Jim sprinted in.

"How is she?" he said, sweat beaded on his brow.

"Grazer and Mendoza are still in with her," Mary blurted. "Bridget will be coming out any minute with an update."

"How long has she been in?"

"Over two hours."

"Do they think they can get her lungs back up?" He was sweating too. He must have driven there straight from his run.

"They're trying." She sounded annoyed. She tried to be patient with his questions, but she was growing angry.

"What do you mean, *trying*?"

"Jim, I don't know!" she snapped. "If you were here, I wouldn't have to explain all this to you. Don't you know how hard this is for me too? And you weren't even here. You are *never* here with us! Do you have any idea how hard this is for me to do alone?"

Jim glanced down at Mallory. She didn't look back at him. Jim looked back at Mary.

"I know." He apologized. His tone softened. "I'm here now." He paused and looked at Mary, who was crying. He held her tightly. She let him. Mary was angry but needed him desperately right now. When her world felt like it was falling apart, somehow his arms always made her feel safe. His arms made her feel like he could protect her from the world. She cried into his arms for a few minutes, and he held her tightly. Then she took a step back and wiped her eyes.

She smiled as she looked down at Aunt Gail's Bible and picked it up.

"Look what Mallory brought." She tried to smile.

"Aunt Gail's Bible?" he answered. "Did you find all the answers?" He gave her a boyish grin.

"Ha, not yet, but I pray I find the answers someday."

"I'm going to go find us some more coffee," Mallory interrupted. "Anyone want anything?"

"Water, please," Jim said. "And thank you, Mallory, for always being here."

Mallory gave Jim a smile and looked at her weary sister. "Mary? Can I get you a refill?"

Mary just shook her head. "I still have this," she said, her eyes pointing to the cold coffee next to her books.

"Okay then," Mallory said. "I'll be right back."

"Mr. and Mrs. Rutherford?" Bridget, the surgical nurse, called to them as she came out of the double electronic doors. Bridget was dressed in green scrubs as she pulled her paper face mask down away from her mouth.

"Bridget!" Mary jumped to her feet.

"Ben and Ava are still in with Jenna," Bridget explained. "Her lungs are severely compromised, and the scarring from all the bacteria is making things very difficult. Ava made two incisions under Jenna's ribs and will be adding drainage tubes. They are hoping that it will allow enough drainage that they can get the lung back up."

Mary and Jim just stared at Bridget, trying to comprehend what she was saying.

"But they can do it, right?" Mary's eyes blazed in fear.

"They're desperately trying, Mrs. Rutherford." Bridget's tone was sympathetic but level. "Over the years, Jenna's lungs have had extensive damage, and her scar tissue is creating serious complications. They are trying to decrease the pressure of the lungs at the moment, but it's her entire right lung that collapsed, not just a section. If the water seal doesn't work, they will have to consider removing a large section of her lung in hopes it's enough. But due to the long-term damage of her lungs, that would be their last resort." Her voice was calm but serious.

"Oh God," Mary cried. Jim didn't say a word.

"I'll come back out as soon as I know more," Bridget said.

"Thank you," Mary said, almost pleading.

"Of course, Mrs. Rutherford." She placed her hand on Mary's shoulder. "You know Jenna's in the best hands with Ben and Ava."

"I know," Mary said, trembling. "But that's my baby girl." Her voice trailed off as she began to cry.

"I promise to come back when I know more," Bridget said as she pressed the large blue button on the wall and the double doors opened. She pushed the face mask back over her nose and mouth and walked in.

Mary sobbed as she sat back down. She hated that she was so used to waiting for doctors. She had waited for hours when they tested their daughter for cystic fibrosis, she had waited all day for lab results, and she had waited for doctors to come out and tell her what surgical procedure they had just done. She hated that she knew everyone at Westchester General by their first name, but she loved her daughter, so she'd wait as long as she had to.

She tried to read her novel, but she just couldn't focus. Unable to sit still, she began to pace around the room, her anxiety reaching outward. The sunset's dimming light leaked past the windows, rays of pale gold and peach spilling into the drab waiting area. Mary's gaze lit on the black book—Aunt Gail's Bible. She picked it up and started flipping through the pages. "Good book?" she huffed. "Doesn't everyone die in this?"

Jim reached over and grabbed her hand and squeezed it tightly.

"Mary, she'll be fine." He seemed to be trying to convince himself. He looked over at Mary, and his eyes grew serious. "I'm so sorry, honey. I'm so sorry I'm not here as much as you need me. It's just—this place breaks me. I feel so helpless. I can't fix you. I can't fix Jenna. I can't do anything here but just sit and wait."

Mary didn't say a word.

"I know it's not about me. But if I can't help you or Jenna, then what good am I? I'm never here because you don't need to deal with my stupidity on top of everything else you have to deal with. If I'm not part of the solution, then I'm part of the problem, right? I don't want to be a part of the problem, *your* problem—*her* problem," he said as he motioned toward the double doors. His voice quieted, and then he said in angry frustration, "And I have no idea how to be part of the solution."

"Just *being* here is the solution," Mary angrily said. "Just be *here*, Jim. That's all anyone one can do. Do you think I want to be here? Do you think I have a solution? I don't! I'm not a doctor, but if she's here," Mary pointed toward the electronic double doors, "then so am I."

She turned from Jim and reached back for the Bible and flipped again through the pages.

Jim hung his head down, his voiced muffled in sadness. "You're stronger than I am, Mary. You always have been." He looked back at Mary, his eyes filled with tears. "I just love you both so much, and I'm so scared. This place scares the hell out of me."

She put the Bible back down and looked at her husband, tears escaping his green eyes.

"I know you lost your parents," he said in a choked voice. "I've never lost anyone I've loved. Ever. And I don't know if I ..." He couldn't continue. He sat there in his own silent sobs.

Mary leaned toward him and paused. She didn't look at him as she said quietly, "You can."

He looked at her face, tears in her eyes.

"I can't live without you and Jenna in my life. I'm scared to death right now." His eyes were swollen and red. He wrapped his arms tightly around Mary and kissed her head hard.

They stayed in their chairs, Jim's arms wrapped around Mary, Mary resting her head on his shoulder.

It was another hour before the electronic doors of the ER opened. This time, Dr. Grazer walked through them. He didn't say a word. His head was down, his shoulders fallen, his steps slow. He pulled the mask from his face and clenched it in his hand. He finally stood before them and drew a breath but couldn't exhale it fully without emotion.

"I'm *so* sorry." Grazer's eyes welled with tears. "We tried everything. Jenna's lungs were too scarred and damaged to expand. We weren't able to remove her lung safely without an available organ to transplant. We tried every possible scenario to prolong her body's ability to wait for a transplant. I swear to you we tried every exhaustible option possible." His head shook hard, his eyes filled with tears of remorse.

"I'm so sorry, but she's gone."

Mary let out a wail as she fell hard against Jim and then collapsed to the floor. Her voice rose, an agonized howl of despair and grief came out. "No!" she screamed, not able to move her face off the cold hospital floor. "My baby! Not my baby!" Her body cradled in a ball as she trembled and cried, her tears evoking the faint smell of ammonia and lemon from the cold tile floor.

Jim covered his face with his hands, and his shoulders shook as he wept uncontrollably. Mary's loud cries filled the room. Nurse Bridget stood in the doorway, sniffling back the tears that streamed down her face.

Dr. Grazer walked over to the security guard. "Please keep the room cleared and let them remain as long as they need to. I'll be back shortly with the hospital chaplain. Right now, I have to go back into the OR and release Jenna to the mortuary."

* * * *

Everyone has their breaking point. Even hospitals.

22  *In the Wake of It All*

*I*t was the first day of September, and Emily Waal was in preschool, recovered from her car accident over two months ago. Tommy was home, skimming his newsfeed online when he spotted a link with a picture that caught his eye. He recognized it instantly. It was Emily's hospital friend, Jenna.

Tommy clicked on the link. It took him a minute to realize it was her obituary he was reading.

Rutherford, Jenna V.—13 of Yorktown went to heaven on Tuesday, August 30

He froze and reread it twice in disbelief. He couldn't believe it was true. He recalled thinking how much that little girl didn't belong in a place like that. She just didn't fit. She was so vibrant, so full of life.

His eyes filled as the obituary listed that her services would be Friday at 2:00 p.m. He sat there a few minutes in shock, then contemplated if he should go or not, contemplating if he *could* go.

Friday came, and Tommy stood in line, the sun beating down on him. He told himself he'd just offer his condolences to her parents and leave. He held in his hand the 2012 shiny hospital penny and a bag of peanut M&Ms. He had a need to bring something.

Tommy was surprised how long the line was. He had gotten there thirty minutes before the listed calling hours, and the line had already looped outside into the parking lot. Standing outside in the long line, he was amazed to see the hundreds of people already there. There were sobs from school children who huddled together, consoling each other, just a few feet in front of him. They were with their parents who were also in tears. He looked behind him and recognized the nurse from the hospital and the security man from the pediatric floor.

What a special girl she must have been to have touched so many lives.

Tommy didn't make it inside the funeral home for another hour, and by that time, the outside line had more than doubled in size. It was another hour before he got to give his condolences to Jenna's parents.

Tommy recognized Mary standing next to a man he assumed was her husband. Both looked exhausted and empty. Mary was in a dark blue sheath dress, the husband in jeans, sneakers, and an ill-fitted tweed jacket. Tommy hugged them both and offered his deepest condolences, and they thanked him for coming.

Not ready to leave, Tommy took a seat toward the back of the room next to a woman in her late sixties reading a Bible.

"You know why life is so precious?" He couldn't help but think his thoughts out loud. "Because death is inevitable."

She just looked up at him for a second and returned to reading her book.

He continued in outward thought.

"Why does it takes such a tragedy like this to see the precious gift that each day holds? Why does it take a death to truly see life?" he questioned. He vowed to himself right then and there that he would not waste another moment. He felt he owed it to that little girl who was so full of life. The older woman just ignored him.

Tommy stayed as he watched hundreds of people pay their respects to Jenna's parents. They hadn't moved the whole time Tommy was there. They seemed to console those who were trying to console them. Tommy noticed that they never stopped holding each other's hand either.

The overcrowded room stretched beyond capacity, and people were standing shoulder to shoulder. The school-aged children even sat on the floor in between the rows of chairs. A low hum of voices and sniffles filled the room.

Tommy looked over to his right and saw Dr. Grazer sitting next to the janitor from the hospital.

The Bible-reading woman hadn't moved either. He turned his attention toward her and extended his hand to the woman. "I'm Tommy. How do you know Jenna?" he asked quietly.

She looked at him and scowled, "She's my niece—my *grand*niece. God rest her soul." She resumed flipping through the pages of her worn Bible.

"We shared, well, my daughter, Emily, and Jenna shared a room at Westchester General back in June," he stated.

"Shh," she hissed. "Now is not the time for idle chitchat."

"I'm sorry. I'm really not sure what I'm supposed to do in this situation. I've never been to a wake before."

"Pray," she said decisively.

"To Jenna?" he asks innocently.

She looked over at him. Her face searched his. "No, you pray *for* her soul to rest eternally with our Lord Savior. Praise God."

"Oh," Tommy said. "Can I ask you another question, Aunt …?"

"Gail," she answered sternly. "Aunt Gail."

"Can I ask you a question, Aunt Gail?" Tommy began. "You seem to know the right thing to do in this type of situation. I'd like to know, what do you think I should do? Should I tell Emily about Jenna or not? She's four."

Aunt Gail jerked her head at Tommy, her face stern. "Absolutely not!" Her voice bellowed. The people in the row in front of them turned around, faces frowning.

She lowered her voice. "Leave the dead to bury their own dead. Go and proclaim the kingdom of God." She closed her Bible and leaned in closer to Tommy. "I have kept secrets to save heartache. Why upset a child with answers no one can give her. What cruel soul would let her go through life wondering … searching for a man who was never there?"

"Man?" Tommy questioned.

Aunt Gail's cheeks flushed. She ignored his question. "Do *not* tell your dear, sweet child. She will live just fine without having to know all of life's cruel pain." She returned her attention to her Bible.

Tommy contemplated what Aunt Gail said and remained in his chair. He looked around the room and noticed the old janitor from the hospital get up and walk up to the small white casket and bow his head in prayer. Tommy could see how distraught the old man was as he talked to himself, shaking his head left and right.

The old man bent low and seemed to be whispering to Jenna. Oswin took off his heavy gold necklace and birdlike charm and placed it next to Jenna. Tommy saw him make the sign of the cross and leave.

Tommy thanked Aunt Gail for her words of wisdom and stood up. Aunt Gail just nodded her head, never taking her eyes off the pages of her Bible. He walked down the hallway toward the exit, his eyes looking at the dozens of picture boards that lined the walls of the funeral home. There were pictures of Jenna in school, laughing with her friends under the heading "St. Bishop."

There were pictures of her riding the teacup in Disneyworld, and her face full of excitement as she plunged with her parents down Splash Mountain underneath a board marked "Vacations." There were boards marked "Friends," "Adventures," and each board had dozens of pictures, all of Jenna smiling.

Under the board titled "Family" hung many pictures. There were new ones and old ones. There was a wedding picture of a young bride holding a bouquet of peonies in her hand. There was a picture of a woman with two young girls, ages ten and two, Tommy guessed, eating a rather large plate of chocolate chip cookies. And there was an older picture of three women standing by a stonewall fence holding drinks in their hands, a sunset behind them.

Tommy studied the pictures, still not believing that such a vibrant young girl had died. He placed his 2012 penny and his bag of peanut M&Ms under the poster board titled "General." So many pictures of doctors and nurses smiling with Jenna. Looking at the pictures, Tommy was convinced she was just one of those things that didn't belong.

He studied the picture board for a few minutes and then walked outside hoping to take a breath of fresh air. The night was still too warm, even for September. He reached into his black slacks to retrieve his car keys. He unlocked his car door and was about to get in when he recognized the old janitor sitting in his car next to his. Tommy tapped on his window.

"Sir?" Tommy asked.

Oswin rolled down his window. "Yah, mon? What it be?"

"Did you know Jenna well?" he questioned.

"Yah, mon."

"She was pretty special? Wasn't she?"

"Yah, mon, tru dat, she be dat all right."

Tommy stuck out his hand toward Oswin. "My name's Tommy," he offered. "I met you at General a few months back. My daughter, Emily, was in room 313."

"Hi ya, mon, me know." He extended his hand back to Tommy. "Me name is Oswin, but me friends, they call me Oz."

"Well it was a pleasure to meet you, sir."

"De pleasure be dat little girl in there. Now go on. Take care of your little one. You a good mon. Don't lose sight o dat now. Go on, now."

Tommy waved good-bye through the window and got in his car and left.

* * * *

Oswin reached over for a card resting on his passenger's seat. He opened up a faded yellow card and read:

Oz, my spirited Jamaican hummingbird,

With this hummingbird charm, you'll always be reminded that you are never far from a home, an owl, and a butterfly.

x,
Vivian

A little piece of paper fell out with it.

Avery's Antiques and Treasures
518 Fleming St., Key West, FL 33040

The doctor bird hummingbird is one of the most outstanding of the 320 species of hummingbirds. It lives only in Jamaica. These birds' beautiful feathers have no counterpart in the entire bird population. In addition to the beautiful feathers, the mature male has two long tails that stream behind him when he flies. The doctor bird remains a colorful national symbol of Jamaica.

He folded everything back up neatly in the envelope. He kissed it and held it up to the sky and prayed.

"Jah Jah, yuh have always been me guide. Me suffering a broken heart. Remind me heart dat love transcends. All me faith and trust is in Jah the Almighty." He bowed his head in prayer. He sat for a moment and let his tears fall. He sniffled a whisper to himself, "Ya, me know Jah, Jah, all be revealed when de time be right."

After a few minutes, Oswin returned the card carefully on top of a pile of old letters stacked and bound together with a yellow ribbon. Each letter was addressed to:

Dr. Alexander Morgan
701 Pauline Street
Key West, FL 33040

* * * *

Some secrets you keep until your grave. Some secrets stay buried even longer. Some people find treasure in what others threw away.

23 *Written in Stone*

*D*r. Ben Grazer walked back to his car after Jenna's graveside service and sat in the driver's seat, the leather hot from the sun. He started the engine to run the air conditioner. He remained in his car until the last person left the hour-long service. Hundreds of people had shown up at the cemetery to place a rose upon the small white casket as it was lowered into the ground. All came to say their last good-bye to a little girl who changed their life.

After Father Fred had finished the Our Father, Aunt Gail had invited everyone at the service to attend the service luncheon at Our Lady of Lourdes church hall. One by one, they all returned to their cars and left the cemetery. Everyone except Ben.

As he watched the last car exit the cemetery, Ben turned his car off and got out, then grabbed a folded chair, a paper bag, and two glasses from the trunk. He walked a familiar path toward the black tombstone by the tall oak tree. He stood in front of the stone, opened the chair, and sat down. He rested each glass on both knees as he poured them halfway with Patrón.

"Today, I need a double," he said to the stone. And he poured a little more tequila into his glass. He rested one glass on top of the stone. From the other he took a long swig and sat back down. A light breeze blew across the cemetery.

"She's gone." He brought the glass slowly up to his lips and took a long mouthful of tequila. He swallowed hard and let out a heavy sigh, then hung his head low as his shoulders dropped. "I couldn't save her," he said as his head shook back and forth in anger.

"Alex. I swear to God I tried. I just couldn't—" His voice broke in pain. Ben lifted his head and gazed at the stone as if it could hear him. His eyes red, he sat there staring.

"I know, you always warned me, 'No more than just a hint of compassion, Gray,' you'd always tell me. But damn it, Alex, I can't help it. I'm not a machine. How on earth did you live with just a *hint*?"

He drew the glass back to his lips and took another long swallow.

"We took the Hippocratic oath, Alex. Remember?" He stared coldly at the stone.

"I swear to fulfill, to the best of my ability and judgment, this covenant." He began reciting the oath to the stone.

"I will respect the hard-won scientific gains of those physicians in whose steps I walk and gladly share such knowledge as is mine with those who are to follow." Ben continued but then stopped, his eyes glaring as he took another gulp of tequila. "Was that your best knowledge you could share with me, Alex? A *hint*, a fucking hint of compassion? I thought the oath said, 'first do no harm.' Isn't that what the oath said? What do you think I just did to that entire family? I didn't just *harm* them, Alex—I *destroyed* them. Can you hear me? I *destroyed* them!" He stood up holding the glass in his right hand, his voice escalating in anger. "We're supposed to *save* people, Alex. I'm supposed to fucking *save* people! I'm not supposed to harm—I'm not supposed to destroy—I can't be you, I can't just do a hint—I love what I do. I love making a difference—I *loved* that little

159

girl. Damn you, Alex!" He threw his glass at the granite headstone, and it smashed into tiny pieces. The glass shards glimmered in the sunlight while he collapsed to his knees and wept, the grass soft under him.

After a few minutes, Ben wiped his eyes with the back of his hand and stood up. He walked over to the stone and wiped most of the shattered glass off the base of the black granite with the sleeve of his suit jacket. He picked up the other glass of tequila from the headstone and poured it on the grass next to his feet. He placed his hand on the top of the stone and said, "Sorry about that, Alex. I'm just broken today, you know? I know I did all I could, but sometimes I just wish I could do more. I care, Alex. I always will." He shrugged his shoulders as he read the tombstone:

Alexander Morgan, MD
July 17, 1949 – March 13, 1987
See You at Sunset

Compassionately, he tilted his head and let out a sigh. "Why did you unbuckle, Alex?" His voice was kind. "We were a good team. You were a great mentor and one hell of a doctor. I'll give you that." Ben forced a grin. "You know, you really are a good listener, and you're probably still my best friend." He laughed at the irony of what he had just said. Ben smiled and raised his empty glass toward the stone. "I'll see you at sunset, my old friend. Until we meet again. Here's to it being many, many years from now."

Ben folded the chair and walked back to his car. He opened the truck and laid the chair flat. He placed the half-empty bottle of tequila in a black bag and shut the trunk. Wiping the sweat from his brow, he took off his jacket and tossed it into the backseat as he started the engine and turned the air conditioner on full blast. He turned the vents toward his face as he waited for the car to cool down. While he waited, he turned on the radio to fill the silence. Tim McGraw's "Live Like You Were Dying" came from the speakers. "Well isn't that just great." He looked over at the red rose on the passenger seat. He had grabbed the rose from Jenna's service and was going to bring it home—a remembrance, he thought, a tangible symbol of something so precious. Sitting there listening to the song, he changed his mind; he decided that love and beauty are to be experienced and embraced, not to be captured and held. He grabbed the rose as he opened the driver's door and stepped out into the late afternoon heat. He walked a few hundred yards until he came upon the newly dug hole. He stopped and stared at the ground for quite a while.

He stood over the small white casket, covered in roses, and prayed. He hadn't done that in almost thirty years. After he finished, he looked down at the casket and quietly said, "You taught me more about life in thirteen years than I ever learned in my fifty years of living." His voice broke as he wiped the tears from his eyes. "Thank you, Jenna. I will never forget you. How could I? I will never forget the lesson you gave, that love always remains." And he tossed his red rose on the top of the mound of flowers.

He stood there for a moment out of respect. Ben was ready to leave when he heard the song of a wind chime close by. He looked over at the five-foot-wide gray granite tombstone to the right of Jenna's. It was well maintained with newly planted flowers, a few small solar lights lining the stone, and a single wind chime that was now playing a soft, tinkling melody. Grazer read the granite family headstone:

Crenshaw

Vivian Elizabeth	Phillip Michael Crenshaw
Reynolds Crenshaw	
2/14/1956 - 12/21/1985	11/12/1953 - 12/20/1985

Loving Parents to

Mary Morgan Crenshaw	Mallory Paige Crenshaw
4/30/1978 –	8/9/1984 –

* * * *

She has my name.

24 *New Beginnings*

*I*t was September 3, and Westchester General Hospital was being inundated with camera crews and media alike. A state senator had a press conference scheduled that afternoon on the front lawn by the aster plants that were in full bloom. She had planned to announce to the media the far-reaching benefits of her newly proposed Child Health Care bill. The conference was moved into the hospital grand foyer due to the unseasonably warm temperatures.

Senator Monica Williams was a polished politician running for president of the United States who had perfected her on-air presence by her second term in office. She articulately expressed to the well-dressed CBS news anchorman covering the event that the whopping $20 million tax bill could now support the much-needed advancement to health care to all those in a hundred-mile radius.

A red MedEvac helicopter approached the rooftop landing. Dr. Mendoza and Dr. Rohn were already on the rooftop, awaiting its arrival. Nurse Ellen was in the middle of admitting a new patient to the third floor, a young boy who just was diagnosed with Hodgkin's lymphoma. His worried parents were lost and overwhelmed. Ellen calmly walked them through the process of admission as she carried the boy's belongings up from the emergency room.

The lights on the third-floor pediatrics flickered when they stepped off the elevator. Ellen looked up at the lights and then over at Sara, who was entering patient information in the computer as she sat at the nurses' station.

"Oh great," said Sara. "We are already on backup generators. Dear Lord, what's in store for us today?"

* * * *

I can see the torment in the mother's eyes. She was lost in more than just the hospital. Her husband was not fairing much better. They were nervously asking Ellen questions, one after another, and she was patient with each answer.

It was then that I felt a cool breeze.

* * * *

At the nurses' station, Sara opened her desk drawer. She grabbed her sweater and put it on. In the room, Oswin was mopping the floor, mumbling to himself, complaining about how you could catch a cold in a place like this. When he finished, he placed the tent card on the sanitized hospital tray. "Cleaned today—General Hospitality #701."

He let the door close behind him and placed a yellow caution sign a few feet from the door. It was then when it started to get cold. Really cold, like a meat locker.

"There, that's better," said a small voice.

I knew that voice.
I knew it well.
It couldn't be.
It can't.
But it was.

"Let's get it cold in here just the way I like it," the familiar voice continued.

"*Jenna?*"

"Yup. You betcha. The one and only." Her voice was as chipper as ever.

"Well, fancy meeting you back here," I said. "I have to say I'm a little bit surprised."

"Really?" she said. "I've spent more time here than anywhere else, and I know this place like the back of my hand—well, you know, when I had one." She giggled.

"Your humor is something else, you know that?"

"Yeah, I've been told. Mr. Oswin used to tell me that all the time. You know him? He's a pretty cool dude. He's been here for like, forever."

"Ha," I laughed. "Sure do. He was my roommate in Key West at 701 Pauline Street, back when I was a young doctor."

"Seven-zero-one? That's his extension here—General Hospitality 701."

"Is it now?" I smirked.

"So wait, you were young? I mean, a doctor? Like my Dr. Grazer?"

"I hired Gray, your Dr. Grazer, here at General a long, long time ago. He'd be lost without me. Why do you think I never left?"

"My sparking personality and irresistible charm?" She giggled, her voice strong with joy. "So, that's a yes? You know him too?"

"I taught him everything he knows."

"Well, you obviously either don't know or forgot to teach him how to play Rummy, because he's really bad at the game. He loses all his peanut M&Ms to me." She paused for a moment. "Or was that your doing?"

"That's true, he's really bad at games, and no that

wasn't me. However, I do make a pretty mean chocolate pudding cup."

"Hey, that's my favorite!"

"I know."

Out in the hallway, Nurse Ellen was explaining to the young parents that the sheets and towels were kept in the blue bin. Their voices were growing louder, and their footsteps were right outside the door.

"So you know everyone here?" Jenna questioned.

"Only the frequent flyers."

"That's what my Dr. Grazer calls me!"

"Who do you think came up with that term? I'm pretty clever too, I'll have you know. Grazer's a better doctor than I ever was. Your Dr. Grazer makes a difference in the lives he touches because he cares with the perfect amount of compassion. He was my friend—he was my best friend here at General." I paused for a moment and added, "Until I abruptly left him at a plane crash in Phoenix."

"Yeah," she said, her voice sad. "I didn't mean to do that to my parents." She was quiet for a moment, then her voice lightened. "But they've gotta know that this bundle of personality can't be contained. I'll make sure that they know I'm okay and that I'll always be around and that I love them. I'll leave them all kinds of signs every chance I get. You see, I've got this *Love From Above* penny thing that I was big on down there. I'm kind of famous for it."

"Who *above* do you think started your collection?"

"You?"

"The one and only."

"No way! Get out of town!"

"Ha, maybe I should, get out that is. Perhaps it's time I leave of this place. Thirty years here at General has been a long time. I've always wanted to go back down south. Back to the coral reef and the warm turquoise water. I have been thinking I might take up sailing. Captain Tony seemed to love that. Maybe I'll head back to 1010 Windsor Lane and help some folks out at my old stomping grounds at Memorial. Maybe Clark is still running the show there. Maybe I'll go down and have a little fun in the Keys."

"And maybe—" Jenna led.

"And maybe …" My smiled widened. "Maybe there's a beautiful blue-eyed blonde in a yellow sundress waiting for me with a slice of key lime pie and a margarita, ready to watch the sunset celebration slowly melt into the horizon. It's been awhile since I've seen her at sunset. I hear Atlantis is beautiful this time of eternity."

Jenna giggled. "You should Instagram that #SeeYouAtSunset and tag me!"

"Insta what?" I questioned. "Tag you? Tag you where?"

She giggled again. "Ah, guess they don't have it up here, do they?"

"His room is right here," Nurse Ellen said to the young, frightened parents. "It's right next to the showers if either of you need to freshen up before I take you back down to the recovery room. If you need extra blankets and extra pillows, they are down the hall here on your left. You both can wait right in this room until he's out of surgery." Her hand rested on the handle of the door. "I'll be able to take you back down to see him when they call me." She took her hand off the door handle and rested it gently on the young mother's shoulder. "He's in good hands here. Dr. Grazer is the best."

"He sure is." Jenna said with pride.

"Yes, he is."

"It shouldn't be too long now," Nurse Ellen said as she returned her hand to the door and turned the handle. "I'll be here until seven." The faces of the parents were solemn. The wife wiped the tears from her face and then reached for her husband's hand and squeezed it tightly.

"First time in, first time scared," Jenna said. "Poor kid has Hodgkin's lymphoma."

"Terrible disease to deal with," I said. After a moment, I asked, "Jenna?"

"Yeah?"

"You sure you've got this?"

As the door slowly opened, Jenna answered, "Sure do, Gramps. I promise to take care of this place just like you did." She said proudly, "This is my home now. I'm Room 313."

Hello,

Thank you for reading See You at Sunset!

If you liked the book and have a moment, I would appreciate a short review on either Amazon or Goodreads as this helps new readers find my books!

Thank you!
-Margarete

BOOK CLUB QUESTIONS

If you're in a book club and want to share this novel, here are some questions to get you started:

1. Did the ending give you closure?
2. What are the different meanings of "see you at sunset" the author wanted to convey?
3. Who was your favorite character? Why?
4. If you could have written the finale, how would you end the story?
5. What surprised you most in the book?
6. Have any of your views or thoughts changed after reading this book?
7. What was the most capturing chapter or scene in the book? Was that necessary or could it have been removed while maintaining the essence of the book?
8. Who really had more than a hint of compassion, Alex or Ben?
9. Given the circumstances, where would you "live" for eternity?
10. Has this book changed the way you view pennies?
11. Do you believe in spirited animals?
12. Was Gail right to keep Vivian's secret?
13. Were you surprised with the twists, turns, and intertwining of relationships?
14. Do you believe in coincidence or do you believe that there are no coincidences?
15. Do the characters seem real and believable?

16. Was there a character who you wished had played a bigger role, and why?
17. Were you engaged in the book?
18. Were there any particular quotes or sayings that stood out to you? Why?
19. What ideas or theme did the author want you to believe or experience?
20. Did the novel broaden your perspective or open up another belief?
21. What did you think about Alex and Vivian's relationship?
22. Did your opinion of the book change as you read it? How?
23. Was there anything you found profound or that struck you as insightful?
24. Did you try to figure out the connections or did you wait until the ending to make the connections?
25. Whose voice in mostly telling the story? Was that the best way or should it have been written from another perspective? Would another perspective have changed the story?
26. Were there any clues or symbolism to guide you to the conclusion?
27. Did you like the characters' personalities?
28. Would you be interested in a sequel with Helen and Grazer, titled *Frequent Flyer*?
29. Did you like the book? If you have read any of the author's other books, how does this compare?
30. If you could ask the author a question, what would it be?

Email MargareteCassalina@gmail.com and see if she is available to join your book club! She is known to answer, reflect, and partake in book clubs that read any of her books.